"Jesus," said the marshal, as the room was beginning to settle. "A Kansas twister would of done less damage."

Groans and curses filled the air. Someone wearily tossed a last bottle over his head, and it hit one of the wheels of fortune, which began whirring.

"By God," said J.J. Bigelow, his eyes bugging at the carnage. "By God, a man could say all Cole City needs to become the garden spot of the whole entire world is good people and water!"

Slocum sniffed, rubbing his side. "Marshal, I reckon that is all hell needs."

OTHER BOOKS BY JAKE LOGAN

RIDE, SLOCUM, RIDE
HANGING JUSTICE
SLOCUM AND THE WIDOW
    KATE
ACROSS THE RIO GRANDE
THE COMANCHE'S WOMAN
SLOCUM'S GOLD
BLOODY TRAIL TO TEXAS
NORTH TO DAKOTA
SLOCUM'S WOMAN
WHITE HELL
RIDE FOR REVENGE
OUTLAW BLOOD
MONTANA SHOWDOWN
SEE TEXAS AND DIE
IRON MUSTANG
SHOTGUNS FROM HELL
SLOCUM'S BLOOD
SLOCUM'S FIRE
SLOCUM'S REVENGE
SLOCUM'S HELL
SLOCUM'S GRAVE
DEAD MAN'S HAND
FIGHTING VENGEANCE
SLOCUM'S SLAUGHTER
ROUGHRIDER
SLOCUM'S RAGE
HELLFIRE
SLOCUM'S CODE
SLOCUM'S FLAG
SLOCUM'S RAID
SLOCUM'S RUN
BLAZING GUNS
SLOCUM'S GAMBLE
SLOCUM'S DEBT
SLOCUM AND THE MAD MAJOR
THE NECKTIE PARTY
THE CANYON BUNCH
SWAMP FOXES
LAW COMES TO COLD RAIN

SLOCUM'S DRIVE
JACKSON HOLE TROUBLE
SILVER CITY SHOOTOUT
SLOCUM AND THE LAW
APACHE SUNRISE
SLOCUM'S JUSTICE
NEBRASKA BURNOUT
SLOCUM AND THE CATTLE
    QUEEN
SLOCUM'S WOMEN
SLOCUM'S COMMAND
SLOCUM GETS EVEN
SLOCUM AND THE LOST DUTCHMAN
    MINE
HIGH COUNTRY HOLDUP
GUNS OF SOUTH PASS
SLOCUM AND THE HATCHET
    MEN
BANDIT GOLD
SOUTH OF THE BORDER
DALLAS MADAM
TEXAS SHOWDOWN
SLOCUM IN DEADWOOD
SLOCUM'S WINNING HAND
SLOCUM AND THE GUN RUNNERS
SLOCUM'S PRIDE
SLOCUM'S CRIME
THE NEVADA SWINDLE
SLOCUM'S GOOD DEED
SLOCUM'S STAMPEDE
GUNPLAY AT HOBBS' HOLE
THE JOURNEY OF DEATH
SLOCUM AND THE AVENGING GUN
SLOCUM RIDES ALONE
THE SUNSHINE BASIN WAR
VIGILANTE JUSTICE
JAILBREAK MOON
SIX-GUN BRIDE
MESCALERO DAWN
DENVER GOLD
SLOCUM AND THE BOZEMAN TRAIL

JAKE LOGAN

SLOCUM AND THE HORSE THIEVES

BERKLEY BOOKS, NEW YORK

SLOCUM AND THE HORSE THIEVES

A Berkley Book/published by arrangement with
the author

PRINTING HISTORY
Berkley edition/April 1986

ISBN: 0-425-08742-5

A BERKLEY BOOK® TM 757,375
Berkley Books are published by Berkley Publishing Group,
200 Madison Avenue, New York, N.Y. 10016.
The name "BERKLEY" and the stylized "B" with design are trademarks
belonging to Berkley Publishing Corporation.

PRINTED IN THE UNITED STATES OF AMERICA

1

Seen from the rim of the high cutbank the stage was only a speck and a cloud of dust as it drummed along the trail to Cole City. The riders sat their horses grimly watching. They were hard-faced men, heated from their hard pursuit, and their horses were blowing and sweated.

"That is them?"

"It has got to be."

The two who had spoken were at the front of the group; the taller, thicker man, who had only one arm, had given answer to the older man's question.

"Kahane, we had better cut leather," said a third man, a man thin in the saddle, almost like a stick under his derby hat that sat straight on his thin head.

The heavy-set man spat suddenly over his horse's withers, and without turning his head said, "We'll breathe 'em. Don't want to founder our horses, for Christ sake." He was riding a big buckskin stud horse.

"We'll have to go like hell to catch 'em before they get to Cole City," another man observed thinly.

"We will breathe 'em," Kahane said again, and squinted at the distant stagecoach. He was dressed in black broadcloth, with a hard-brimmed black hat on his dark head. His black eyes lay deep in their sockets. His right hand, holding the reins loosely on the pommel of his saddle, was capable-looking, smooth, and very white. The left arm of his coat was tucked into his pocket. He had big shoulders.

"You sure it is them? Bigelow and the kid?" asked a man wearing a long duster coat and a beaver hat.

Kahane didn't bother to answer.

"Smart, Bigelow taking him on the stage," the man with the derby hat observed. "Throwed us off for a bit."

"Excepting they'd be in Cole City now if they'd picked fast horses," said the older man sitting his horse next to Matt Kahane.

Kahane spat again, and cut his eye quickly at the gray-headed man beside him. "Not a chance," he said, his eyes swinging back to the disappearing cloud of dust. "Bigelow knew damn well we'd think they took horses. That's why he took the stage. Look at the time we've already wasted!"

"Well, let's get going then!" someone said. "They're about out of sight!"

"Shut up!" The deep gutters in Kahane's long cheeks seemed to deepen in shadow. Suddenly his face twisted in a grimace, and he bent his head. Reaching to his coat pocket, he brought out a flask, looked at it briefly, and with his one hand unscrewed the stopper, then tilted it and drank. Relieved, his face cleared and he stood up in his stirrups, his eyes intent on the bare horizon. "We'll cut down by the Butte, then across Crazy Creek; and we can likely make it in ahead of them about the time they hit the long grade at Twin Rock." When he dropped his full weight back into his saddle, his horse took a step. "You men, you follow my lead. Don't speak to give yourselves away. Could be passengers aboard and we don't want that kind of trouble. Use your bandannas."

"All we want is that son of a bitch Kincaid," someone said.

The gray-headed man kneed his roan horse close to Kahane's big buckskin stallion. "Matt, remember we're taking him back for trial."

"The man's a rustler, Barney."

"Matt, he's a kid. Not more'n sixteen, seventeen. It's his brothers we really want."

Kahane suddenly let a grin spread across his face, but it did not reach his eyes. "Denny Kincaid'll be the honey for the flies, Barney. Though maybe the lesson would be better," he said as he turned the buckskin.

"The lesson? What do you mean, lesson?" asked Barney. He ran the palm of his hand along the side of his round face. But Kahane had already kicked his horse ahead and didn't answer.

"Hanging's too good for the Kincaid sons of bitches," said the thin man under the derby hat, and he let out a hoot.

"But..." Barney Traherne started to speak, but his effort was lost as Matt Kahane booted the buckskin into a gallop and the posse followed suit. In a moment they were strung out, riding hard for Twin Rock.

Overhead, the pale Wyoming sun stood right at the center of the high, wide sky.

"Hyah! Hyah!" The stage driver's sharp command cut the high mountain air, the echo abruptly cut off in the cracking of the long whip as it crossed over the bobbing heads of the lead team, snaking back to crack again over the wheel horses. The through-braces creaked, the sweating horses lunged into their harness, running into the narrow canyon. Dust rose in a blinding cloud behind the coach's wheels, enveloping the little spotted saddle horse tied to the rear of the Cole City stage. The iron tires rang against the rocky road as the driver's big voice urged his team.

Inside the coach the four passengers were thrown against each other, the three men and the girl giving all their attention to holding their seats.

With an even greater lurch of the Concord as it dashed down into the canyon, John Slocum suddenly found himself almost on top of the girl seated beside him.

Her gasp had hardly broken from her when he had turned to apologize, pulling himself straight at the same time.

"'Scuse it, miss. Looks like our driver's having a rough time skinning those animals."

The big man with the green eyes and raven-black hair caught the rush of color in her smooth cheeks, the flash of anger in brown eyes shadowed by a bower of soft brown hair. It was the first time he had seen her directly and looking really alive; until then she'd been little more than a cold, pale, silent profile sitting rigidly beside him. But the plunge he felt in his insides at the sudden contact of her womanliness brought him into a fresh contact with himself. It had been a while since he'd had a woman that good-looking. The pickings back in Junction Crossing's Cabbage Patch had been pretty well used; but here, suddenly right next to him sat a fresh young girl who couldn't have been a day over twenty-five; beautiful, in fact, and utterly female. And for that wonderful moment John Slocum realized how much he'd been missing. Why, it was a whole two weeks since . . .

But the stage had lurched again, this time throwing the girl against him. In the scramble to maintain her balance she put out her hand which, to his delight, fell right into his crotch. There was nothing more a gentleman could do under the circumstances, he realized, than to take her firmly by the shoulders and set her upright on her seat. At that point, the road became suddenly smoother.

She was seething with indignation and embarrassment, and now sat firmly in her seat, staring straight ahead with the sort of dignity only the young and the old seem able to muster. Slocum liked that.

Across from them the prisoner remained silent, lurching loosely with the coach as he stared down at his manacled hands hanging between his legs. He looked to be little more than a boy; smooth-shaven, with high cheekbones and widely spaced eyes. His hair was long, yellow, and thick and he had bony shoulders. Denny Kincaid was the youngest of the Kincaid brothers, still half a boy, but pushing to be a man. Slocum, passing through Junction Crossing, had picked up news of the Kincaids and their troubles with the Cattlemen's Association, and how they had all four of them broken out of the Junction jail and gotten clean away, save for Denny, who'd been caught and brought back. But there had been talk of lynching.

Seated beside the boy, the stringy lawman with the longhorn mustache and knobby jaws was looking for a place to spit.

Slocum watched the man's dilemma with amusement. The floor wouldn't do, not with the girl there, and he

5

was obviously fearful of the window, not wanting to let fly into the wind. Slocum was toying with the notion of telling him to use his hat when, with an incredibly sour face, the leathery man swallowed painfully and continued chewing, though at a slower pace.

"Company gives little thought to their passengers, and that is for sure," the lawman observed now, covering his discomfort with the observation. There was a drop of moisture on the end of his long nose.

"How long do you think it will take us to get to Cole City?" the girl asked, refusing to look at either the prisoner or Slocum, but with her eyes directly on the man in front of her. It was the first time Slocum had heard her speak since he'd picked up the stage outside Junction.

"I'd allow another hour or two, miss." The stringy man coughed suddenly, phlegm rattling in his throat, and Slocum watched the drop of water fly off his nose. "I know this country, miss. I see you're a stranger. Yes, I'd say an hour." He sniffed, his pale eyes watering. "Name is Marshal J. J. Bigelow." His glance included Slocum. "Sorry about this here, young lady." He nodded toward the prisoner seated beside him. "But necessity takes us to Cole City, in the interests of justice. Got to get him into a jail he can't bust out of, like him and his brother done at Junction; nor vigilantes bust in."

"D-Don't you count on th-that, M-Mister Marshal m-man," said his prisoner, stammering hoarsely. He raised his head only high enough to stare unabashedly at the girl's bosom. Slocum's own eyes roamed pleasantly toward his seat companion's firm, prominent breasts.

The boy continued to speak to those two beauties. "This old m-man f-f-figures he's g-gettin' me to Cole C-C-City so's that vig-vigilante m-mob won't lynch me 'f-fore the judge g-gets a cr-crack at it." Though his eyes were still firmly on target, he was clearly seeing something else as he spoke, seeing the picture he was relating. *Well,* thought Slocum, *hanging after all is no joke,* and he could understand the boy's inability to really see what his eyes were looking at. Pity.

"Well, M-Mister F-F-Fancy M-Marshal," the youthful prisoner continued, "I will be long g-g-gone from that C-Cole City jail 'f-fore that b-b-bunch of ki-killers even f-find I'm shut of Junction!" He grinned as he looked up, his young face opening suddenly as though he was seeing his three companions for the first time since he'd started to speak. He was a nice-looking young fellow, Slocum thought, but not too young to have his neck stretched.

A snort rode down J. J. Bigelow's long nose. "You reckonin' on your brothers coming for you, huh? Listen, boy, let me tell you somethin'; they'll be dancin'—all you Kincaids will be dancin' air—well, by time the first snow starts to fly. Exceptin' it's gonna be legal. So stop your fancy talk, and be thankful J. J. Bigelow is kindly toward the young, even though a young squirt, by God, and done his duty, and is still doin' it, by God, savin' you for the judge to deal with legal." And, shifting his long weight, his big hand brushed the big Navy Colt at his hip.

"My br-brothers will b-b-be comin' f-for me," the boy insisted.

"And J. J. Bigelow will be waitin'!" the marshal said. "I will be waiting for them or anybody else takin' a notion to runnin' the law theirself!" He snapped his hard jaws together and touched the Colt with his long, hairy forefinger.

Slocum waited, half watching the side of the girl's face, the curve of her bosom, the smoothness of her thigh, but studying the lawman and his prisoner too; thinking of the Kincaids busting out of the log cabin lockup at Junction, getting clean away; all save young Denny, whose horse had suddenly decided to head north and west, while Denny headed south. Denny had been clapped back in jail pronto. But tempers had demanded action, and while the posse was out chasing the Kincaids, another group began to form with the idea of carrying out justice on Denny and saving the circuit judge the trouble and what's more, setting an example for those rustling Kincaids and other maverickers, by God!

Slocum was wondering why Bigelow had chosen to take young Kincaid by stage rather than on fast horses. Trying to slicker the lynching party, no doubt. It must have been a tough decision to make, and it took guts, moving the boy to Cole City.

"I'll b-be out of your t-tin c-c-can jail 'f-fore you can turn the k-key in the l-lock," the boy was saying. "Not that a-a-a one of us K-Kincaids ever t-took anything from a honest m-man in this c-country; b-but we know not a—not a one of us c-could look for a fa-fair trial f-f-f-from any damn circuit j-judge the Association would allow to ho-hold c-c-court."

Slocum sighed. He'd heard it all before. The big brag. At the same time, he knew the Kincaids were quite capable of getting their brother out. They were a tough bunch, not the type you could backwater. Nor was Marshal Bigelow, either, it was plain to see. But the marshal was in no enviable position, caught between the Kincaids and the lynchers. It looked like the old boy might be digging his own six-by-six. Slocum watched J.J's chew-

8

ing suddenly speed up as the coach slowed now, coming to a long grade. The teams lay into their harness while the passengers settled into their seats.

The girl had not spoken again. In all, it had been a fairly silent trip since Junction Crossing. Slocum wasn't sorry. For though he would have liked talking with the girl, he found his thoughts were occupied mostly with Nat Cullen and the reason for his visiting Cole City.

Cullen's letter had caught him in Cheyenne. The information had been sparse, like Cullen. "Hello, old friend. Looks like Little Round Top out here by the Flint. I never did pay you back that bottle of Indian River whiskey."

It was unsigned, but Slocum knew it was from Cullen; the reference to Little Round Top told him the nature of the action his former army companion was engaged in, and the Indian River whiskey told him that the situation contained everything from rattlesnake tongues to bear piss, and watch it. Flint River meant Cole City. But it was the fact that Nat Cullen had called for help at all that told Slocum the gravity of the situation.

Leaning forward, Slocum put his head out the window to check the spotted pony. He had decided to take the stage at least part of the way to Cole City in order to arrive with a rested animal, figuring to drop off before coming into town so he could ride in from another direction unnoticed. A man never knew when he was going to need a fresh horse.

When he sat back again he found Bigelow's shrewd eyes right on him.

"How come you didn't pick fast horses instead of the stage, Marshal? If you're trying to beat out a lynch posse, the young lady and myself here could be included in the party if things should get lively."

A mirthless grin touched the corners of Bigelow's eyes and mouth, and quickly vanished. "The boys won't figure us on the stage, least not right away. I'm hoping to win some time."

"I already know that's what you figured, but if they catch up with us, hoping isn't going to help."

Bigelow blinked, then shifted his chew. "Other reason is Denny here; he has trouble with the horses. Gets throwed just about every time he climbs onto one of them animals. Damnedest thing." He swung his long head toward his prisoner. "Ain't it so, boy? You and the hosses. Always been that way." He looked over at Slocum again, raised his thick gray eyebrows, and dropped them.

Denny Kincaid had been regarding his captor with his lips in a tight, straight line. Now, without looking at the girl, he spoke to her. "D-Don't listen to the old man, mi-miss. He is t-t-trying to get me m-mad so's I'll jump him and he c-can sh-shoot me with a ex-excuse. Huh— B-Bigelow!" He looked straight at the girl now and smiled shyly. "Me and the hor-horses g-get along just f-fine, m-miss."

J.J. must have felt he was losing ground, for he came on strong now. "Folks in these parts does not take kindly to stealing cattle and horses." He sniffed hard. "And neither does the law, and neither does J. J. Bigelow." He half turned toward his prisoner, who had moved away from him. "Reckon that message will get through to those dumb brothers of yourn?"

"We di-didn't steal any ca-cattle and we di-didn't s-steal any horses," the boy stammered back, his smooth cheeks and forehead coloring.

"Only from about every outfit in the valley, by golly.

Cut it out, Denny boy." The marshal squinted across at Slocum and the girl. "Just a week back, found twenty head of fresh-changed brands on the Kincaid range. Couldn't find clearer evidence if you made it yourself." He sniffed. "You are too dumb and mebbe too crazy to know what those brothers of yourn bin pullin' off all these years."

He looked at Slocum and the girl, tapped the side of his head with his forefinger, and rolled his eyes, sighing deeply.

"I dunno. Reckon the boy is slow." Young Denny didn't appear to notice this observation.

"Sh-shi . . ." He stared to say when, swift as a striking rattler, Bigelow cut him off.

"You watch yer language there! You are in company of a lady!" J.J. tipped his hat. "I apologize for the prisoner, miss."

"I would suppose," the girl said suddenly, "that it would be up to the judge, or whoever the appropriate authority is, to decide the matter. Anyhow, I don't consider it any of my business; or interest."

J. J. Bigelow gulped, almost swallowing his chew. The prisoner's eyes went blank, and Slocum let out a burst of laughter.

"Owe you one there, miss," he said with a big grin.

But the girl wasn't having any. She just sat there, saying nothing further, and Slocum felt his laughter bubbling up again. By God, she was a corker!

"Back home I remember the girls all said John Slocum was going to grow up to be a ladies' man. Guess I should've stayed home." He cocked his eye inquiringly at the delightful wisp of brown hair that was just touching the color that had risen in her cheek.

"John Slocum's the name, miss."

"I had already figured that out, sir. Now, if you will excuse me . . ."

But Slocum decided it was time to straighten things out. "Miss, you are real smart; by golly, you are smarter than my old schoolmarm. And I don't mind a little sociable sassin', but don't you think it's time you got down off that picket fence before one of those sharp points does you damage?"

Her gasp of anger came at the same instant as the red flush filled her face, and she turned to him with her eyes flashing fire. But before she could say anything a shot rang out and a loud, harsh voice called out for the stage to pull up.

"Got us on the rise, by God, when we can't run the horses," said J. J. Bigelow as his hand swept to his hip.

"Better not!" Slocum's voice cut the marshal into a freeze. "You're not going to be anywhere near fast enough," he said; and he nodded to the window, where a scattergun was pointing in at the four of them.

"Everybody out," said the voice. And it was clear its owner was not going to argue.

12

2

Quite suddenly the sun had paled behind a wall of gray sky that had slipped down from the Absarokas, and there was a coolness sifting the air. The four passengers lined up outside the coach with the driver who, while keeping his attention on the masked men, was also alert to his horses, who were stamping and snorting, ready to spook at the slightest provocation.

"I don't want them bolting," he said, his tone surly. He was a short man with long arms, thin, with a sharp nose and two teeth missing in the front. Slocum noticed that he smelled of neatsfoot oil.

"Keep an eye on them, then," said the one-armed man on the big buckskin, who was obviously the leader. Like all the others, he had pulled up his bandanna to cover his face, except for his eyes.

"There ain't no box," the driver said. "We ain't carrying anything. So what do you want?"

"It's him we want," the man in the derby hat said, and the one-armed man wheeled on him with an angry gesture to be silent.

Then, looking directly at Denny Kincaid, he said, "Him!" His voice was muffled.

"Take him, then," the marshal said. "I done my duty."

Denny Kincaid's face was sour with anger. "You b-buggers afraid to sh-show your f-faces. Hell, I-I-I know wh-who you are!"

"Shut up, Denny!" snapped Bigelow. "You're in enough trouble already."

"Th-thanks f-f-for t-tellin'."

"Throw your guns and belts over there." The man on the buckskin indicated a spot not far from the coach. When this was done he said, "Don't follow. We'll be checking our back trail. This kid is getting what's coming to him. And his brothers will get it next." He spoke over his shoulder. "Bring that dun horse."

Slocum had said nothing, had simply watched, trying to place the men in his memory so that if necessary he could recognize some of them later. The one-armed man, obviously the leader; the one with the old Derby hat who had spoken out of turn; the gray-headed older man who was sweating a lot.

"Thoughtful of you to bring a horse along," Bigelow said.

It was a brisk little dun with a wide white blaze on his forehead and three white-stockinged legs. One of the masked riders dismounted and checked the rigging, tightening the cinch.

Suddenly the girl spoke. "What are you men doing? Why are you taking him? Who are you?" She turned to J. J. Bigelow. "Marshal Bigelow, who are these men, and why are they taking your prisoner?"

"They're going to lynch him, miss."

"No!" The word broke from the gray-headed man

whose mask was beginning to slip. Realizing this, he held it up with one hand as with his other he pulled on the reins of his horse to quiet him.

"Shut up!" snapped the man on the buckskin. "Kincaid, get up on that horse. Hurry it!"

But the girl had taken a step forward. "You can't do that. You mean, they're going to hang him? Without a trial?" She turned again to Bigelow, her face working in astonishment as the realization of what was happening broke on her. "Marshal Bigelow, arrest them!" And she looked suddenly at Slocum. "Do something, for heaven's sake!"

"Miss, there ain't nothin' we can do against those guns." Bigelow reached out and took her arm as she started forward, but she pulled away from him.

It was at that moment that Denny Kincaid put his foot in the stirrup and swung his leg over the dun horse. The dun dropped his head and started to spin. Denny stayed with him; but then the horse stopped, planting all four feet hard, almost shaking his rider loose, and then began to buck and spin at the same time. The boy landed flat on his back on the hard ground with the wind knocked out of him. He lay there grunting, trying to suck in air.

"Like I told you," J. J. Bigelow said, chewing fast on his tobacco. "Him and the hosses, uh-uh!" And he reached out and grabbed the girl's arm as she started forward again. "He's all right, miss. Just shook some."

It was just at this point that the leader of the posse reached into the pocket of his coat and pulled out a metal flask. The action caught Slocum's attention immediately and he felt his breath catch as he watched the rider unscrew the cap and take a drink.

"Something the matter, mister?" The voice coming down from the buckskin, though still muffled, was hard as a gun barrel as the black eyes met Slocum's steady look.

"Isn't the kid a bit young for hanging?" Slocum said as the man on the buckskin horse returned the flask to his pocket. "Why don't you pick on someone your own age?"

"Watch it!" Bigelow said swiftly at his side, his words sharp with warning.

"Matt, you promised..." The gray-headed man started to say. But before he could get out another word, the big man smashed the back of his hand against his face. "Shut up, you lily-liver!" He spun the buckskin and shouted, "Get him on that horse! Tie him on if you have to. Hurry!"

He sat hard as a post on the buckskin while two men loaded Denny into the saddle, and then two others on horseback flanked the boy and the horse so that he couldn't fall off, one of them holding the dun's reins.

"Let's move! You men pick up all the guns. We'll dump 'em along the trail. They can find 'em." He glared down at Slocum. "And you, you better mind your own business!"

"That is just what I am doing. And I asked you a question, mister!" Slocum was feeling the anger all the way through him now, but mostly he was concerned that none of the posse take note of the spotted horse tied to the back of the coach. The Winchester was on the far side of the pony, but if someone rode over they couldn't miss it.

He could hear J.J.'s breath whistling out of him as he braced the man on the buckskin, but the lawman didn't say anything further.

The leader of the posse had booted the buckskin forward until the big animal was right up against Slocum, who didn't move an inch. "I said stay out of it!"

"Mister, you can consider me right in the middle of it!" He was thinking of the silver flask in the other man's coat pocket.

"I will see you around then, by God!"

"You sure will," Slocum promised.

"I can't go along with this." The gray-headed man's voice was shaky, but he had his courage as he cut in now, still trying to adjust his bandanna.

The other man jerked the buckskin's head. "Then go on home. We're dealing with cattle stealing, and you had better know it, and so had the Kincaids better know it!"

A man off to Slocum's right suddenly shouted. "Hey, what about that pony there, looks like—"

But before he could say another word, Slocum, who was standing close to the girl, let out a war whoop and, reaching over, pinched her as hard as he could on her buttock.

Her scream of fury drowned out his whoop, and brought everyone's attention to her as she smashed Slocum in the face as hard as she could.

"Jesus!" J. J. Bigelow's jaw dropped in admiration of the power and speed of the blow. Slocum felt as though he'd been hit with a rock. But it had diverted the attention of the posse for the moment.

"Ride!" shouted the leader of the party. "Move it! God damn it!"

Someone cursed, and the jangle of bits and creak of leather filled the air.

"Anyone follows, we shoot!" And, with some hooting and hollering, they raced off.

The girl was still furious as she charged Slocum, who was quickly checking the rigging on the spotted pony.

17

"You beast! How dare you! You filthy swine!"

"I'm sorry, miss, but I had to keep them away from my horse and rifle." He could see it made her even more furious that he was ignoring her, giving his attention to his horse.

Bigelow strode over to him. "Slocum, I am the law here, and I want that horse."

"You wouldn't be wanting to ride after them, would you, old-timer?"

"That kid is my prisoner, and they are going to stretch his neck pronto.

"Sorry, Marshal."

"Slocum, I order it. I am the law.

Slocum shoved the rifle back into its scabbard.

"You a lawman, Slocum?"

"Lawman? No. I am my own man." He stepped into the stirrup and swung onto the horse. "I'll see you along the trail or in Cole City," he said. With a nod at the girl, who was still glaring at him, he kicked the spotted pony into a gallop.

He had a lot of questions; the main one being how that son of a bitch on the buckskin horse had come into possession of Nat Cullen's silver flask. Cullen had carried that through the war. It had saved his life once, deflecting a Yankee bullet from finding its target. Slocum was sure it was the same. It had that dent in it that Nat used to sometimes rub with his thumb after he'd taken a drink.

The trail was easy enough to follow; they had no reason to conceal their tracks. But he could tell a good deal about the men he was following. They were careless. Someone had dropped a bandanna; someone else had lost a tobacco tin. Slocum had learned early always to take care of his back trail. You never knew when someone just might come along. These were careless men, fools, but nonetheless dangerous.

At a place where a deer trail crossed he found his handgun, and Bigelow's and the stage driver's. It wasn't long before he caught up with the posse. Riding up a draw, he saw the still-warm horse droppings; he could hear the posse now. In a moment he rode to the lip of the pocket valley and, looking down, saw them close to a creek lined with cottonwoods. Concealed by some bullberry bushes, he had a good view of the action.

They already had a rope and noose hanging from the branch of a big cottonwood. Denny was sitting the dun horse, while one of the posse held the animal close up so he wouldn't move. The boy's hands were tied behind his back. None of the posse now wore masks, and Slocum had a clear view of the one-armed man on the buckskin. That tight, bitter face was one he would not soon forget. He watched the others now, gathered in a semicircle. The boy was glaring defiantly at his captors, not showing fear so much as anger.

Slocum hesitated, making sure he'd counted all the men down there, sure that there was no outrider posted who could surprise him. Then he slipped down closer, leading his horse to another bullberry bush. Settling himself, he calculated the firing distance. He had no plan. One against twelve were odds that trusted more to luck or divine intervention. He could hear the men speaking clearly.

"Make sure that horse don't move," the leader said now as, still on the buckskin, he placed the noose over young Kincaid's head.

Slocum watched the boy's eyes close.

"Damn it, Kahane, if we're going to do it, do it, and let's get shut of it," said a man with a heavy black beard. "What are we waiting for?"

Kahane checked the knot. "Now you men draw back and leave him set there on the horse." He kneed the buckskin away.

"Somebody's got to spook the horse so he gets a drop, for crying out loud," someone said.

"No. No. This boy's going to sweat for it. And whoever finds him will tell the others, the Kincaids and all of them, how we done it." He looked around at the semicircle of sweating faces. "He's going to sit there and wait. Now you men move out slowly, quietly. I don't want any noise."

"Jesus!" someone said.

Another man coughed out a grim laugh.

"You mean, let him set there till the hoss takes a notion to move? Might be a while."

"Might be," Kahane said. "Might be a bit of a while."

"Matt, are you sure?" The man with the heavy black beard had kneed his horse over to Kahane. "He's just a kid, you know."

Slocum could tell the bearded man was only asking for his own sense of right, not because he disagreed with the decision.

"Kahane, you cannot do this...not without a fair trial!" It was the gray-headed man again, but some of the other men glared at him now.

"Barney, we are doing it to teach them rustling scums a lesson." Kahane's cold black eyes covered the group. "Also, I see some of you have got queasy all of a sudden. Don't cotton to hanging rustlers. So I'm doing you a favor. You don't have to watch. See. Just ride out and go home. You didn't see nothing."

"Kahane..." The gray-headed man started to say.

"Drop it, Barney. Leave it." The venom packed in those words carried all the way up to Slocum. Already he was counting the odds. He had the Winchester, and not very good cover; and there were twelve of them. Not much in odds for him.

"Ask the kid if he has some last words, for God's sake!" The man named Barney almost screamed the words. But he didn't wait. He rode right up to Kahane, his face scarlet in its combination of outrage and pleading. "Matt, please; we've got to wait for a trial!"

Slocum could see every line of the contempt on Kahane's face as he sat looking at the older man confronting him. A moment passed, and then he turned to the boy.

"You want to say anything, Kincaid?"

The boy started to try to speak. He was scared now, and nothing came out, only his silent stammering, stammering over words that made no sound at all, words which in their silence were more terrifying than if he had screamed them.

Kahane turned the buckskin. "Ride out slow," he said to the men, "and silent."

The man in the derby spoke to the man beside him, and Slocum heard him. "Good. It will teach them all a lesson. We'll sure enough get rid of the Kincaids and all the damn rustlers."

His companions, riding slowly to the creek at the edge of the pocket valley, nodded and voiced their agreement. All save the older man, Barney, who sat slumped in his saddle, letting his horse take him along with the others, wherever they were going.

Slocum could still find no opening to make a play.

Never had his attention been so keen. Each detail of the tableau before him was totally vivid. The horsemen reached the bank of the creek, which was lined with willows and more cottonwoods. The moment was prolonged in a nearly unendurable length, like the stretching of a note from a harp in the wind: the slow procession to the creek, the boy waiting on the horse with the noose around his neck in the dying afternoon sun. A held breath that couldn't last.

_ One of the riders drew rein and looked back. Others followed suit.

Slocum felt something twisting inside him as the posse waited for the dun horse to move. Or for life to continue. But the tableau remained breathless. For that unendurable moment there was no life and no death down there at the cottonwood tree. There was no time.

Then suddenly the man named Barney straightened in his saddle and let out a tremendous Texas yell; at the same time drawing his handgun and firing it into the enormous sky.

"God damn you!" screamed Kahane.

But he was drowned out by the other men shouting and firing their guns as they wheeled their horses and pounded, still firing, across the creek and away from the grim little valley, away from what was being done.

In the same second that the dun horse started forward, Slocum pulled the trigger of the Winchester. He saw the rope snap and the boy fall from the horse.

He waited, ready for them to ride back, but no one had noticed. His shot had been covered by the general firing and excitement. In a moment he was on his horse and racing down to where Denny Kincaid lay on the ground. The boy was unconscious, but he was breathing. He was alive.

When he got back to where the stage was waiting, Bigelow was standing by the horses talking to the girl, while the driver was asleep inside the coach.

"I was getting close to unhitching one of the team to go looking for you," the marshal said.

Young Denny had regained consciousness along the way, and Minton, the driver, gave him a drink of whiskey, which he kept for emergencies, or anything else. It almost gagged the boy, but it brought him around.

"Jesus," Bigelow exclaimed when he saw what the rope had done to the boy's neck. "That is what you call a close shave, and I don't mean a joke there, boy."

The girl, meanwhile, had found some ointment in her belongings and rubbed some of it on Denny's neck. He said nothing; only his lips trembled now and again, as Slocum had seen them do before, but no sound came out. In his gray eyes there was a blank staring, unnameable and not easy to look at. Leaving the girl and Denny out of earshot, Slocum related the details of the slow lynching to Bigelow.

"The buggered bastards!" exclaimed J.J. "Christ, what's the matter with people like that?"

"I got a good look at them, Bigelow."

"I know who they are," the marshal replied. "For whatever good it'll do," he added ruefully. "Do you reckon I can arrest the whole bunch of them?"

"You can arrest the ringleader. You can arrest the one named Kahane."

"Don't tell me my business, young feller!"

"Then don't ask."

The marshal spat vigorously at a clump of sage and said, "Like you to take on as deputy, Slocum. I could use a good hand siding me. You're sure ornery enough."

Slocum grinned wryly at the old man's effort at reconciliation. "I already told you I wasn't a man of the law."

"A man can sometimes change his mind."

They had returned to the girl now.

"I'd say he needs a lot of rest," she told Bigelow. And then, turning to Slocum, "I presume you are all right, Mr. Slocum."

"I presume you are, miss."

"I'm Rhonda Haven," she said, coloring. "I suppose I should introduce myself."

"Well, cool is better than cold, my grandma always told me."

But he saw she wasn't going to let go any further. Her eyes glanced off his face and she turned back to Denny Kincaid, who was sitting inside the coach. He had still said nothing.

"Think his voice is gone?" Bigelow asked.

"I think he should see a doctor as soon as possible," the girl said. "His neck could be injured inside."

"There is a doc in Cole City," Bigelow said. "Or was when I was last there. You never know about the population in that town."

The driver had hitched his horses now and swung up onto the coach. "We'll make it soon enough if you folks can do your gabbing inside," he said sourly, scratching his armpit.

Slocum was studying the delightful dimple at the side of Rhonda Haven's lips.

"Will you please drive carefully?" she asked. "I mean the bouncing around."

The little stage driver scowled and said nothing, as the girl and Bigelow climbed inside.

Settling himself, J.J. said, "Only it ain't him that has to be all right, and sure not his neck. I wouldn't want to be in that posse's shoes when the Kincaid boys gets aholt of what happened. Kahane, he is tough, but there is three of those Kincaids."

"So you won't need me as deputy, old-timer," Slocum said, and he laughed, standing outside the coach and leaving his hand up on the window frame. "You've got the Kincaids to help you straighten that lawless posse."

Bigelow grumbled some kind of answer through the open window, but Slocum didn't hear it. He was looking back down the trail to make sure there was no one. Suddenly the girl was at the coach window.

Looking up, his eyes met hers for a brilliant instant, and then she was again closed to him. Slocum felt the warmth all through his body.

"Will they come back?" she asked.

"They could. But we won't be here."

He swung up onto the spotted pony and nodded. The stage driver cracked his whip and the coach jerked forward. Slocum rode quickly toward Cole City as the afternoon light lengthened, and the colors of everything in the land and in the sky became other colors and still others.

He was thinking of J. J. Bigelow offering him a badge. Clearly, things were going rough in Cole City. Where did Cullen fit in? Which side of the law was he on? Like himself, Nat was the kind who could take his pick either way. And it might not be so easy to locate his old friend if things were this tight. And how did that son of a bitch get Cullen's flask?

But he would be seeing Bigelow again; maybe he would start with Bigelow. He grinned at the tips of his pony's ears as he kicked him into a brisk canter. The sun felt good on his shoulders and back, and on the backs of his hands. He felt good all the way through.

3

The town lay like a buzzing bee in the bronze light of late afternoon. On the surrounding plain the grass crackled as all the things of the land stretched toward the coming evening. An eagle suddenly swept the naked sky; somewhere on a back street a dog barked.

Cole City was mostly wood, save the bank and jail, which were brick. On Main Street the sidewalks were eight feet wide, while the streets were covered with grass. A recent town ordinance prohibited buffalo and other wild animals from running at large in the streets.

After the tents and lean-tos the first building to appear had been the San Francisco House, moved from nearby Holyville. Cole City was still being built. The town sang to the music of saw and axe and hammer, not to mention the bawling of cattle and the not-infrequent crash of gunfire. There was the ordinance against carrying firearms in town, but then there was also the law against fighting and drinking in the streets and running your horse.

Slocum had taken a room at the San Francisco House,

had bathed at the Barber & Bath down the street, and had changed to fresh linen. Now, with a lighted havana in his hand and an adventurous look in his eye, he strolled along Main Street watching the life, reflecting on how he would go about finding Nat Cullen. And in the back of his mind was the hope of running into Rhonda Haven.

Yet he forced his thoughts away from the girl. He had come to Cole City on business; not that pleasure was to be ruled out, by any means, but he had to keep sharp. Cullen just had to be mixed up with the cattle trouble, and Slocum knew that he would be targeted himself, and pretty soon now. He couldn't afford to relax for an instant, or he was as good—or as bad—as dead.

The sun was almost down and a chill had come into the air. He had decided that rather than go actively looking for Cullen he would wait and see what he attracted. He wanted to get the tempo of the town, to feel its tone, meet some of its people and learn their temper. Right now Cole City was a town blistering with dissension, ready to break out into warfare over the eternal problem of maverick cattle branding, and so definitely not the sort of place for a stranger to come in asking questions, especially regarding someone of the character of Nat Cullen.

He knew that sooner or later Cullen would find him, or he would hear or see something that would give a lead. And, if necessary, he could initiate an action that would start something without the appearance of his investigating anyone's business. Cullen could very well be on the run, hiding out. It was appropriate to wait.

Slocum hadn't been around this long without knowing how to be patient, how to take advantage of whatever came to hand. Some who had experienced this quality in him claimed it was Indian blood; he was said to be part Cherokee. Some said it was just plain grizzly.

Pausing now, his eyes fell on the sign posted outside the Pick-Em-Up Saloon announcing that Reverend P. P. Dillman of Holyville would preach there that Sunday; on conclusion of the services a horse race, a cock fight, and a pie-eating contest would take place. Taking a last look at the busy street and the rich sky, Slocum walked through the swinging doors.

The room was large, smelling of coal oil, cigars, chewing tobacco, spittle, whiskey, and men. The mahogany bar ran almost the length of one wall. Behind it a large mirror allowed the clientele to regard themselves or each other if they so wished; or they could watch their backs—always a sensible activity. On the other hand, there was the massive nude painting which from another point of view could be said to be more interesting; certainly it attracted a good deal of conversation.

The liquor met Slocum's standard, not trail whiskey by any means, flavored with rusty nails and snake heads, but the real thing. He leaned with his back lightly against the bar, ready for fast movement, and let his eyes rove over the room. There were three monte tables, two wheels of fortune, four or five card games, and there was faro and a big dice game down at the far end of the room. A balcony ran along two walls, and there were doors visible, through which women and now and then their patrons entered or emerged.

In a corner of all the activity a fiddler, a piano player, and a man with a drum offered the sound of music. Some of the patrons were dancing in an adjoining room which, while sufficiently spacious for pretty close dancing, had no room for the musicians who remained in the gaming part of the establishment. With the door open, it was a satisfactory arrangement.

Picking up his drink, Slocum moved down to the other end of the bar so that he could watch the crowd around the dice table. His eyes now fell on the broad back of a man watching the dice game. He was a big, heavy man, solid in a tight, muscular way, and wearing a blue hickory shirt and red galluses. He had red hair.

Suddenly he turned and his small, sharp eyes instantly picked up Slocum, but rested on him only for a moment, a moment that held a question. Slocum simply let his own eyes drift, while taking full note of the red-headed man.

Casually, he turned back to the bar, and with his hat-brim low he watched the man in the mirror. Yes, no question he had been recognized. And that was all right. Everyone must already know about Denny Kincaid. He was probably in jail. Bigelow wouldn't have been se-cretive about his prisoner, wanting people to know there was law and order.

Slocum was letting his eyes glance around the mirror as though looking at the room. But he could see the red-headed man looking his way every now and again. And now, watching the big redhead moving through the crowded room, saying a word here and there, he realized he could be the manager or proprietor.

Slocum downed his whiskey and crossed over to the crowd at the dice table. He had the feeling that action was called for.

He quickly spotted the house man running the game, a bony, wet-looking individual with gartered sleeves, bright yellow galluses, big suspicious-looking cuffs, a chest like a chicken's, ferret eyes, and a pair of hands like quicksilver. He was wearing a silk top hat. His name was Pony de Cob and it took even Slocum with his sharp eyesight a good while to spot Pony switching tops and flats. He handled the dice like lovers, and he was raking it in for the house. Pony couldn't lose, except when he intended. Since the tops never threw a six-ace seven, and the flats were straight, all the little man needed was nerve, talent and those smoky palms to make the switch. He could have given odds to a rattlesnake and beaten him.

At the moment Pony was slickering a group of young cowhands from the Turkey Track outfit. Slocum had seen the red-headed man nod to him, and figured it was the signal for Pony to strip the drovers. The boys were liquored, and Pony was doing a professional job, letting them win just enough to stay in. Slocum worked his way right to the edge of the table and saw Pony de Cob cut a quick glance to somebody behind him. He didn't turn around to see if it was the big redhead.

"How about a roll, stranger?" The little man tossed the dice to him.

For a moment Slocum held Pony's ferret eyes. "Good enough." He picked up the dice. Good. It was the opening he'd known would come sooner or later.

The little man covered a couple of his throws with solid bets, the cowboys just tagging along, Slocum losing one and winning the other.

When Slocum passed the dice back, Pony came out with a nine. He immediately offered to borrow on the six-ace draw for fifty.

"On nines and fives I always bet on the make," Slocum said.

"I'll make it for fifty."

"Make it for a hundred," Slocum said, and he laid down the money and pushed it into the pot. A stir of excitement ran around the table, and there was some jostling. One of the cowboys emitted a low whistle.

A tight grin cut across Pony de Cob's face as he called, then made his throw.

Slocum reached out and picked up the dice, and as he threw them back to de Cob he said, "Two hundred you don't make it."

Pony counted out the money while the crowd around the table froze into silence.

It took the little man four throws to make his point. A murmur went through the crowd as he reached for the dice.

But Slocum beat him to it, sweeping the dice into his big hand. "A win like that, a man would reach for the pot, wouldn't he? But you grab for the dice." Under his silk hat, the little man's face turned scarlet with anger.

"What are you saying there, mister?" And he started to reach for the money at the center of the table.

"Leave the pot." Slocum's three words fell across the table like three bullets.

Nobody moved. Then a chair scraped along the floor somewhere. Somebody coughed.

"What the hell you think yer doin'!" The little man finally found his voice. "I made my point!"

Slocum's hard green eyes bored into him until he dropped his head and looked around at the gaping cowboys. "What's goin' on with this feller?" The words whined out of his thin face.

Suddenly Slocum was aware of the crowd opening to his right, and the red-headed man was there, accompanied by two other men Slocum had seen him talking to earlier.

"What's going on here?"

Slocum held up the dice. "Man here is palming tops and flats, excepting this time he just wasn't quick enough."

"Red, this here feller is full of shit!" Pony's whine cut like a knife scraping on glass.

"Let me see those." Red held out his hand. Slocum offered only a cold grin.

"Uh-uh. Get the marshal. We'll let him take a look."

"I run this place. The name, mister, is Weber."

"We will wait for the marshal. You can send some-one."

"Mister, I don't take orders from you. Hand over those dice. This is my place. You understand?"

"Red, let me handle this." It was the man to Weber's left, a beefy bruiser with a black stubble over his jaws, big hands, and narrow eyes.

"This one's my pleasure, Bruce." And Red Weber took a step forward, reaching out with his left hand, while his right moved slightly toward his hip, enough to brush back his coat to expose his holstered gun. "The dice. I want to see them."

Slocum was well aware of the large space that had rapidly cleared around himself and Weber and his two henchmen. All to the good, for he was going to need plenty of room for movement. "I am not armed," he said. "Like the sign said, I checked it at the door."

"I don't give a damn whether you've got a gun or not. I want those dice."

"Only proving that they are crooked," Slocum said. His eyes swept the gathering. "You boys get that!"

"Mister . . ." Weber's hand had moved closer to his holster.

Slocum grinned suddenly. "Here's Marshal Bigelow now," he said, raising his voice loudly. "He can take a look. You couldn't throw a six ace with them if your life depended on it."

Red Weber didn't even blink, knowing it was a ruse, until Slocum suddenly threw the dice right in his face. It was enough. In that split second Slocum was up on the table and had kicked Red Weber right in the jaw, knocking him to his knees, and without a pause in his movement had thrown himself at one of his companions, smashing him in the throat.

Weber lay on the floor clutching his face, his hands covered with blood. Nearby, Slocum drove his knee into the third man's crotch. The man named Bruce let out a gasp of agony. As he tried to raise himself, Slocum smashed his fist into his neck. It was a perfect rabbit punch. Bruce's head dropped like a stone.

Instantly, the cowboys had joined in and the entire room was in an uproar. One of the cowboys delivered a wicked chop between Pony de Cob's little eyes, dropping the dice man like a roped steer, then drove his elbow into the solar plexus of another, who fell as though his legs had been cut from beneath him.

By now the entire room had become a welter of pugilistic fury. One bartender was protecting the merchandise with a bungstarter, laying out customers right and left. One of Weber's men had appeared with a gun at the side of his risen boss and the roaring Bruce, only to be cut down with a flying chair. Another chair hit Slocum in the back, driving him to his knees. But he rose and smashed three swift punches into Red Weber's kidneys.

The red-headed man fell in agony to the floor, his eyes bulging out of his head. Everyone was throwing punches, furniture or bottles and beer mugs. The bartenders kept shouting for order, but one was smashed with a flying bottle, and his companion, swinging the bungstarter to good account, was finally brought down by one of the cowboys throwing the cash register at him.

Red Weber was again on his feet, now pulling at his holstered sixgun. Somebody screamed, and Slocum, who was too far away to grab Weber, suddenly reached down, lifted Pony's inert body, and threw him at the big redhead, who staggered, giving Slocum time to charge. Swinging punches furiously, he punished Weber to his knees and finally, with a tremendous right uppercut on the point of his jaw, knocked him cold.

All at once the musicians charged into a brisk rendition of "The Star-Spangled Banner." One man heard it and, stopping in the midst of the free-for-all, stood at attention, rigid with patriotism, if not liquor, but only for an instant as a flying bottle caught him and he sank in alcohol and patriotic blood to the floor. His assailant was immediately cut down by a flying chair which did double damage, also smashing Bruce, who was struggling to his feet, right in the back of his neck. Slocum had fought his way to the door, to be met by a furious J. J. Bigelow, who was only then arriving on the scene.

"Been waitin' for you, pardner."

"Nice to be expected," rejoined the marshal wryly. "I'll be wantin' you for a witness, and I might even say you be under arrest."

"Then you better arrest him," Slocum said, nodding toward the inert Weber. "He started it."

"Jesus," said the marshal, as the room was beginning

to settle. "A Kansas twister would of done less damage."

Groans and curses filled the air. Someone wearily tossed a last bottle over his head, and it hit one of the wheels of fortune, which began whirring.

"By God," said J. J. Bigelow, his eyes bugging at the carnage, his jaws working fast as the wheel of fortune. "By God, a man could say all Cole City needs to become the garden spot of the whole entire world is good people and water!"

Slocum sniffed, rubbing his side. "Marshal, I reckon that is all hell needs."

He lay on the bed in the little room at the San Francisco House, staring up at the big water stain on the ceiling and at the peeling wallpaper where it met the corner above the window. It was hot, even with the window wide open. It would cool off soon, for he hadn't been in the room very long, and the heat had collected inside during the day. He lay on the bed now with nothing moving other than his breath and his thoughts.

It was all right lying there. It was good. He could just let the tiredness circulate through his bruised, aching body. His eyes dropped down to the damp-looking curtain hanging limp at the side of the window. He smiled at it; it was just how he felt following the fight at the Pick-Em-Up Saloon: limp, damp—just hanging there.

When he heard the step in the passageway outside he reached over and drew the Colt from his gunbelt hanging on the back of the chair.

The knock on the door sounded male, decisive, yet not like the law. Thing was, you never knew. There were all kinds of knocks in this country, like all kinds of people.

He didn't answer, and the knock came again. Slocum swung to his feet.

"Slocum! John Slocum!"

The voice was a man's, smooth, with a Southern accent; insistent. For a second he wondered if it was Cullen disguising his voice, but then he heard, "I'm a friend. Quimby Hounds. Colonel Quimby Hounds of the Cole City *Finger–Gazette*. I have news for you, sir. Would you open the door?"

With the gun in his hand, he stepped to the side of the door, turned the key in the lock, and opened it.

The figure standing there was puffing on a big cigar; a pair of dazzling blue eyes regarded Slocum with great interest. On second look, Slocum saw that somewhere within the baggy white suit was an erect, elderly man of considerable dignity. He must have been seventy. Slocum saw traces of the soldier, the actor, the riverboat gambler. The blue eyes twinkled. The flowing mustache and the flowing hair on top of his head were snow white. He carried a malacca cane, the cigar clamped next to a signet ring on his middle finger, and wore a Confederate cavalry hat on his regal head. The total effect was one that made Slocum smile agreeably. He was reminded of an opera he had seen in Virginia City a year before.

"Am I addressing John Slocum, sir?"

"That is correct. Come in...uh...Colonel."

The figure advanced with not a trace of indecision. Slocum stood aside, locking the door, slipping the gun back into its holster. His hand waved to the one chair in the room as he sat himself on the edge of the bed.

"I am obliged, sir," the visitor said. "Let me offer my credentials. I am originally from Mississippi, and presently am editor and publisher and very often principal scrivener of Cole City's great newspaper, the Cole City *Finger–Gazette*. Let me add, that I am the founder of the unique publication." He reached into the sagging pocket of his white linen coat and brought forth some folded brown sheets of paper. "I have brought you, sir, our latest issue."

"Is that why you came to see me, Colonel?" Slocum asked, knowing full well it wasn't.

The colonel turned smoothly to check the door, and settled himself in his chair. "I have come with news. Uh—not so by the way, Mr. Slocum, may I offer you a very fine havana? I have them sent all the way from Denver." And he reached again into a cavernous pocket.

Slocum raised the cigar to his nose, pressing it between his fingers to test it for freshness. "Hmm."

"I see you are a connoisseur of the good things— cigars, wines and spirits, and, uh . . . women?" Colonel Quimby Hounds's long face folded like a freshly laundered serviette into an extraordinarily jovial expression. "Allow me, sir." He struck a lucifer and held it, while Slocum bent his head to accept the flame.

The bed creaked as he sat back. "Good." He took the cigar out of his mouth and studied its lighted end; then he regarded his visitor, allowing his eyes to wander over the elegant face which, though lined, maintained a sound vigor and color.

"You remind me of the redskins, sir." The colonel's deep, plangent voice filled the room. "I mean the way you take your time sizing up a person. Admirable!" He released a wet laugh which developed into a cough and, whipping out a large red bandanna, he wiped his mouth vigorously. Then he sat back in his chair, puffing from the exertion.

Slocum waited. The old boy had something definite on his mind, and there was no point in rushing him.

Hounds's voice was soft now. "I bring news of a mutual acquaintance, Slocum." His blue eyes, surrounded by a faint pink laced with little red lines, and protruding slightly, moved up and down Slocum's face.

"From Washington?" Slocum asked wryly.

"From Nat Cullen, sir. And Nat did tell me that you had a sense of humor."

"Where is he?"

"Not too far from death's door."

"Where is that?"

The voice was a throaty whisper, but still carried power. "Right now, I don't know. He's maybe been moved. I've been watching for you for some time. But I wouldn't put it beyond the realm of common sense to have a try at the Kincaid ranch up on the North Fork. However..." He held his hand up swiftly. "You are probably aware that the Kincaid brethren—all God-fearing folk—are no people to mess with."

"I have already met one of them."

"Young Denny. Yes, our equestrian hero. He is apparently safely in Cole City's jail, under the lock and key of Marshal J. J. Bigelow."

"I expect the news is all around town."

"Little if anything, sir, escapes the eagle eye or ear of the *Finger–Gazette*." A wry smile found its way into the colonel's wrinkles. "I heard of that delightful passage-at-arms, sir. Pony de Cob has long had it coming to him. But, speaking of spirited waters—which we weren't, actually—may I suggest that we remove ourselves to a more favorable atmosphere for conversation? I offer the Elkhorn, directly across the street. We will not be overheard. And it will do no harm for either of us to be seen in the other's company, since I am, after all, a news-hound. Heh-heh." And he stood up. "You will accept my little joke, eh?"

Within ten minutes they were seated at a table in the Elkhorn with a bottle between them.

The Elkhorn was an establishment on the more economical side than the Pick-Em-Up; there was some gambling, but no wheels of fortune, only two poker games and a faro dealer. No dice, no monte.

"Marshal Bigelow, I understand, was not pleased at the caper at the Pick-Em-Up," Hounds said as his hand rested gently around his glass.

"That little bastard de Cob had it coming, and so did that big bastard Weber," Slocum replied pleasantly. "The owner of the place, I reckon."

"Red Weber—yes. Weber's actually foreman of the Box Circle, but he is also Matt Kahane's lieutenant, and as such fills in at the Pick-Em-Up."

"And who is Kahane the lieutenant of?"

"Sir Archibald Tyrell of the Chelting Land & Cattle Company of Cheltenham, in Jolly Olde England." The colonel rolled the words off his limber tongue, carefully pronouncing each syllable. "And he is in residence at the Box Circle up on Easy Creek."

"That's the Association, is it?"

"That's the guts of the Association, the Cattlemen's or Stockgrowers' Association. It consists of half a dozen outfits, of which Chelting's Box Circle is the biggest."

"And Kahane works for Tyrell."

"On the nose, sir!"

The colonel lifted his glass. "Kahane runs the gambling in town; he takes his rakeoff. He has guns, power, all the necessary. He is the ideal . . . uh . . . regulator for the Stockgrowers'; for Tyrell, that is to say. And Weber is his man."

"And the small outfits; they're fighting back."

"You know the story. It is ubiquitous in our time. It is progress. Ah, the great God Progress! The building of the heroic West! It is being built, sir, with buckets of blood and shit! Civilization advances in its customary fashion over the corpses of the victims and the lies of the victors." The colonel had colored, his voice had risen, and he began to quiver.

"Take it slow," Slocum cautioned, touching his arm.

"Thank you, sir. At my age. Well, I have some more years, but at the moment, don't get me started! I say, don't let me get started on those venal sons of bitches! Not that I am against money and power, sir. I love 'em. But these skunks are not only venal, corrupt, not to forget uncultivated. They are far worse; they are stupid!" He bared his teeth as though in pain, or perhaps he was yawning. His teeth looked remarkably sound, Slocum thought. "But don't get me started. Just don't get me started!"

"And Cullen? Where does he fit in?"

The colonel snorted. "He did fit where it hurt the buggers the worst; right up their ass!" He sniffed. "They came to regret ever setting eyes on Mr. Nat Cullen."

A grin worked its way across Slocum's face as he listened to the colonel. He knew how impossible Cullen could be; he had a special talent for angering everybody, no matter whose side they were on.

"I don't know exactly how it came about," Quimby Hounds was saying, "but suddenly Nat was working with the small cattlemen. And before a cat could yawn they'd got him elected sheriff of the county."

Slocum's eyebrows lifted at that. "Sheriff! That's digging it where it hurts. How'd the Association stand for that?"

"Well, it was an election, run by the Kincaids and the rest of the small outfits. Well, you see, they are small but they are numerous. By golly, they threw a political rally the likes of which would've made San Francisco jealous with envy!"

"They counted noses and they pulled a fast one."

The colonel leaned forward, his voice low as an undertaker's. There was the whisper of a smile at the corners of his mouth; his blue eyes sparkled as he touched Slocum's sleeve. "They not only counted, they re-counted, and re-counted!" He shook with silent laughter. "Tyrell and Kahane were out of the country then, down making some deal in the Panhandle for longhorns, so the gossip has it. Anyhow, time they got back, the election was over. Weber alone was ineffective."

"How long ago was this?"

"Less than a year."

"They didn't take this lying down, Tyrell and Kahane."

A chuckle started deep in the colonel's chest and took a while to work itself up to his throat and break out in laughter, which he tried in vain to suppress, glancing quickly around the room as he did so. "They first of all appointed a town marshal, or got him appointed through Cheyenne or wherever, maybe Fort Lassiter. It doesn't matter."

"Bigelow?"

"Not Bigelow. Fellow named Clyde Allnut. Swift with a gun. Tough. Only thing was, he wasn't very bright."

"He tangled with Cullen, did he?"

"Nat—you'll find this out for yourself—Nat was running a little business on the side up around Chance Creek with his lady friend." The colonel really did lower his voice now, and Slocum could hardly hear him. "I won't go into the details. Fact is, I don't know them. But Nat, he was running some cattle that had suspicious-looking brands. I am telling you the story. I do not have my hand on a stack of Bibles."

"So he and this feller Allnut crossed."

"Allnut put lead into Nat Cullen, and what he didn't get into him a bushwhacker did, not long after. Nat looks like a colander with enough bullet holes in him to whistle if he stood out naked in a wind."

"And Allnut?"

"Nat didn't have to waste a lot of lead on him."

Slocum grinned at that. "And then Tyrell put Bigelow in as marshal?"

"Wrong. The government appointed Bigelow. The circuit judge wangled some kind of order, I dunno how it was, and it doesn't matter. Bigelow was sent here as deputy to calm everyone down. He's only been here a short time. Transferring Denny Kincaid over here from Junction is his first action, I do believe."

"So you've got an elected sheriff and an appointed town marshal. J.J. really is in the middle, with Tyrell and the Stockgrowers on one side and the Kincaids and small outfits on the other."

"Bigelow is a good man, I guess. But foolish in that he is—or tries to be—honest."

"Does Bigelow know Cullen's still alive?"

"I don't know. But Kahane is still looking for him."

"Who was the bushwhacker?"

"Could be anybody ordered by Kahane. Or even himself."

Slocum sighed, thinking of Nat Cullen's silver flask. Then he said, "J.J. did show his guts, bringing Denny Kincaid over from Junction."

"He is old. He is not what he used to be. He used to be something, I have been told." The colonel was fingering his glass of whiskey thoughtfully.

"Yes, I seem to remember something about him. Somewhere. Someplace or other," Slocum said. "He's got to be a good sixty going on seventy."

"I have heard it said that J. J. Bigelow can chew faster and spit less than any man this side of the Mississippi," said Quimby Hounds, and his blue eyes sparkled. "It is good to know there are sometimes some men of talent on the side of the law. Though they don't generally last long."

"Some of them go back and forth," Slocum said. "Sometimes the law is a floating game of monte."

"You ever ride with the law, Slocum? Hope you don't mind me asking there."

"I ride with myself, Colonel, and right now I'm trying to locate Nat Cullen."

"You want me to get word to him you're here."

"You say he's out at the Kincaid spread."

"Maybe!" The colonel lifted a rigid forefinger. "They were going to try moving him. Don't know if it's possible."

"But he sent you."

"Wanted me to watch out for you."

"You can tell the Kincaids I'll be riding out to see Cullen—and them too, if necessary."

44

The colonel's eyebrows shot up into his heavily wrinkled forehead. "Just like that, eh?"

Slocum stood up. "Just like that is the only way, Colonel."

4

He was thinking of Rhonda Haven when he walked into the San Francisco House lobby. But there was a tall, rangy blonde. She had just turned from the desk and was walking toward the stairs with her room key in her hand. Tall, though not as tall as himself, with long blond hair, wide shoulders that set off breasts that were all any man could hope for. With each step she took they proclaimed their firm, bouncy resilience. As she put her hand on the wide banister, a certain brilliance seemed to pervade her. She moved smoothly up the stairs with almost no effort, then paused—and he knew it was for him to get a good look at her firm back and buttocks molded delightfully into her tight yellow dress. She was gorgeous.

Slocum stood still in the middle of the faded, dusty lobby under the big chandelier that had come originally from Denver, watching the girl with open admiration as she ascended the long stairway and disappeared onto the floor above. She took her time.

47

When he finally reached the desk and accepted his key, the clerk, without looking directly at Slocum, said, "I believe it's number ten." He had hardly moved his lips.

"In the neighborhood, then. Good enough." Slocum placed a silver dollar carefully on the counter.

He was still grinning to himself when he reached the landing above. There was no sign of the girl, but he noted that the corridor turned a corner only a few doors down to his right. His own room was almost directly ahead of him.

He had just put the key in the lock when he heard her.

"Excuse me, sir. I wonder if you could help me? I don't seem able to work my key."

"Be happy to help a beautiful young lady in distress, miss." And, taking the key from her hand, he led her down the corridor.

"These old locks are sometimes difficult," he was saying. "Though sometimes one of these keys will open other doors."

"How strange! You mean you could go into other rooms with that key?" She was looking at him with an expression of teasing disbelief on her face.

"Sometimes." He grinned. "Like this one here," he said suddenly. "Let's try this one." And before she could say anything, he had put the key in the lock. "Doesn't work."

"But—but suppose somebody was in there?" Now there was a note of alarm in her voice. "My room is around the corner. Number ten."

But he had stepped over and slipped the key into another door. A man's voice came bellowing through.

"What the hell you doin'? Who is that?"

"Sorry. Wrong room." With a grin, Slocum continued along the hall. "Let's just try one more."

"You're . . ." But she didn't say it. The look of amusement on her face had given way to alarm. "I think you'd better give me back my key. I'll try it myself."

But he had already opened the door. "Empty. When I checked in, the clerk told me there were a lot of vacant rooms and I could have my pick, so I did check some of the numbers already," he told her calmly.

She was standing in the doorway watching him as he stood inside the room.

"Come in." And quickly he stepped forward and took her hand.

"Let go!"

But he had pulled her in and shut the door behind her; releasing her hand, he quickly locked it.

"Mister, let me out of here. I've had enough of this funning!" But before she could open her handbag, he had grabbed it and dumped its contents onto the bed.

"Cute little Remington," he said, picking up the tiny pistol. "I see you travel prepared."

Her eyes were flashing and her lips were tight as she spoke. "A girl never knows when she'll run into some crazy person like yourself."

He had pocketed the pistol and stood in front of her, with a cold smile on his face. "What's the matter? Don't you think this bed's as good as yours?"

"I don't know what you mean."

"Get your clothes off and I'll show you."

Suddenly she dropped her haughty approach and with her lip curling glared at him. "Go fuck yourself!"

"Wasn't the idea to fuck each other?" He took a step

forward and she retreated. "Wasn't that the plan? To get me into bed, and then Kahane's boys could come in. Honey, that one is so old it oughta be in a graveyard."

"That's where you're going to end up, you smart bastard!"

But he could see her mood changing, and suddenly her eyes dropped to his crotch. "You've got me wrong, mister. You were right, though, about my wanting you. The minute I saw you in the lobby, I knew what I wanted. I just couldn't help it. But the rest, it isn't true."

"Play it any way you like, honey. But we'll do it my way. Get your clothes off."

Her eyes had moved up to his belt buckle, and now again dropped to his erection, which was pushing wildly at his trousers.

"You do have a convincing argument there," she said, and her voice was softer as she reached up and began to take off her clothes.

She was down to her chemise when she said, "Aren't you going to take yours off?" She moved closer to him, reaching out with one arm on his shoulder while her other hand found the great bulge in his trousers.

He said nothing, but began helping her out of the rest of her clothes until she was completely naked.

He had removed his gun belt and his hat, and now while she unbuttoned his fly his own hands played over her strong, very white body.

Standing in front of her, he felt the firm resilience of her nipples against his chest. Her breasts were full, just the size for his hands. As were her buttocks, he soon found, reaching them as she straddled his hard organ. Now she slipped her arms around his neck and, lifting one leg, brought her heel up into the crack of his buttocks, bending slightly as he slid his penis into her soaking wet vagina. In a moment she had both legs around him and was pumping on his huge member as he carried her to the bed and laid her on her back, neither of them missing a stroke.

"Oh my God..." Her moan came from her whole pumping body, while he drove his tongue into her eager mouth, meeting her thrusting tongue. And now, with her legs almost totally around him, her heels nearly up to his neck, she squirmed and pumped and moaned until he thought he would explode.

They rode more quickly now as she dug her fingernails into his back, then into his pumping buttocks. And he drove all the way up into her, high and hard, pushing against the limit of her as she cried and begged him to come.

But now he slowed his stroke, moving slowly, while she whimpered in her exquisite delight, still begging, still demanding it. Now he drew his great shaft right out to its head until she grabbed him, locking her legs around him. "No, no! Don't go away! My God! I can't stand it! Give it to me. For God sakes, give it to me, Slocum!"

Now they rode faster and faster, thrusting deeper as she opened even more. Sobbing, clutching, yet not losing the rhythm for a single stroke, they moved even faster, thrust and delved and danced their passion to its only possible conclusion.

She lay exhausted in his arms, murmuring, "My God, I've never, never felt this way in my life!"

After a moment Slocum raised up on his elbows. "Next time you want to try it again, maybe you can beat your record," he said.

"I want a next time," she said.

"There's no time like the present," he said, rolling over on top of her.

"Oh my God, Slocum," she murmured. "Where the hell have you been all my life?"

"Right now I'm between your legs," he said as he drove his new erection into her.

"And I'm right with you," she whispered, almost unable to get the words out as again they began their marvelous rhythm, going almost as long this time. Afterwards, resting, dozing, he thought he heard something in the corridor outside.

In a moment he was up and dressed, but there was nothing outside when he looked.

When he came back into the room, she was still lying inert on the bed.

"You got a name, honey?"

"My name's Honey," she said sleepily.

He grinned at her and closed the door on her laughter.

The flat-chested waitress with the sharp red nose took their orders for coffee. When she left them, Bigelow tilted his chair back on its two hind legs.

"I ought to by God order you out of town! I mean— God damn it!" J.J. slipped the palm of his left hand inside one gallus and surveyed John Slocum, who was seated opposite him. They were in the Hello Eatery on Main Street. "If it wasn't for what you done with Denny Kincaid, I would, I swear I would!" His eyes protruded like the knobs on a set of harness hames, and seemed to Slocum just as brassy. "You got more nerve than a horny tomcat on a Saturday night in May, for Christ's sake! Who the hell you thinkin' you are, walking into the Pick-Em-Up and slam-banging the shit out of the place?"

Slocum smiled at the red-faced marshal. J.J. was so angry that even his big mustache seemed tinted with red. "Marshal, I was just pointing out to those poor young cowhands that that dirty little dice man was slickering them to a fare-thee-well. You know you yourself surely have got a rule in town against stacked decks, cutters, blue specs, and tops and flats in your dice games. What they call back East in those big monthly magazines, crooked gambling. Hell, Jesse James hasn't done any worse than that little bastard Pony de Cob."

"All right, all right, shit take it!" The marshal of Cole City leaned forward, beckoning to the waitress. "Alice, bring us some eggs an' some steak, an' more jawbreaker. Might as well wreck the whole of my guts as part," he grumbled when she'd moved out of hearing. He had moved his chew to the other side of his mouth. "Now listen to me, Slocum. You are in big trouble. You cut down Big Red Weber like that, you got to know you are cutting down Matt Kahane. You mind me? You met him! That one-armed son of a bitch on the buckskin stud. It's Kahane runs this here town!"

"First, the son of a bitch is long overdue to get cut down," Slocum said, bearing down on the words. "And anyway, I thought the marshal ran the town, Mr. Bigelow." He finished off his speech with his face looking like a fresh-baked apple pie.

"Jesus, Slocum! That is all I can say! I have had this job shoved up my ass and now I got to handle it. You think you could do better?"

"Sure."

"How?"

"I wouldn't have taken it in the first place." Slocum put down his cup. "J.J., I am not riding you. I appreciate

53

the six-by-six you're in, and I have seen what you've done to be straight with the law and Denny Kincaid. But you can't fight the whole Cattlemen's Association; you can't backwater those big outfits. You are just asking for a lead coffin without the necessity of getting yourself buried."

He paused, eyeing the older man. "On the other hand, your position isn't all that bad."

"How so? How do you figure that, for Christ's sake? You just told me what a mess I'm in."

"It's like this," Slocum said. "Somebody has got to play it straight. They know that; Tyrell and them, and the maverickers, the Kincaids and their bunch, they know it too. Sure, I know they'd gun you down quick as a fart in a windstorm, but they also don't want a whole passel of deputies or the army coming in here."

"I threatened to call in the army one time," J.J. cut in. "Course, I am not empowered to do it, but it threw them some. I mean, for about five, ten minutes."

Slocum had been studying it a moment, looking down at his knuckles, which were still skinned from the battle in the Pick-Em-Up Saloon. "Actually, J.J., you're in a pretty good spot, because they need you. As long as you are here, no one can say there's no law and order, so they'll see to it that you stay."

"That is what I am saying."

"But it is like that on paper, when they're talking. But they can stop talking, and when they get hot you have to watch out. Some asshole can get sweated up and take a shot at you, blame the other side. You get me?"

The old man was shaking his head. "I know. I know."

They fell silent then, each going over it in his own mind.

"They're building up to a showdown," Bigelow said, emitting a long sigh. "Pretty damn quick now." Reaching into his pocket, he drew forth his tobacco, sliced off a generous chew, and put it into his mouth. Socking it into one side so that he had a big lump in his cheek, he said, "How would you like to take on as deputy, Slocum? I could use a—"

But Slocum was already shaking his head. "I already told you no. This is not my fight."

"You saved Denny Kincaid's ass. And whether you like it or not, it is your fight."

"No. I have my own business here."

"Such as." And suddenly those big brassy eyes were pinpointed on Slocum, who under their meaningful stare had to grin.

"You are a sharp lawman, Bigelow, I will say that. But that is my business."

"You a lawman?"

"You already asked me that question."

"That's no answer."

"Mister, as far as I am concerned it is."

Bigelow gulped after running into that stone wall. "You hunting bounty?"

"Neither one," Slocum said, now in a more agreeable tone. "I am minding my own business."

Bigelow canted his head now, squinting at the man seated opposite him. "You know the dice, and I'd allow you could handle the cards pretty slick too, but that ain't your way of life. You handle that gun, but you don't come off like the road agent type. And right now you don't give the look of the law to anyone as perceptive as yours truly. I ain't seen your face on any flyers. But I have heard your name. I know, I know. Rumor. But where there is smoke there is fire." He paused, looking down his long nose at Slocum, who simply sat there quietly meeting his eye.

"Actually, I am here to spread the gospel of love," Slocum said, remembering the sign he had seen outside the Pick-Em-Up. "I'm hoping to listen to that come-to-Jesus talk they've got coming on Sunday."

"I know if you expect me to believe that you likely do figure the whole world to end up kissing each other's ass," Bigelow said. He turned and drove a huge streak of spittle at a nearby cuspidor. "Shit!" For he had missed, hitting the wall.

"Beautiful!" roared Alice, the waitress, coming up. "Who is going to clean that up?" She stood, thin and bare as a broom handle, glaring at J.J., her red hands on her skinny hips.

"Should have your spittoons better placed," Bigelow grumbled.

Slocum looked at the girl's flat chest and thought for a moment of Rhonda Haven.

"I see you like the girls, too," Bigelow said, ignoring Alice, who had stormed back to her counter. "And who don't, eh?" He chuckled. "But you don't look like that feller who was importing 'em from Kansas City. Course, you do put me in mind of someone . . . our former sheriff. He was kind of like yourself, I'd say. Quick with a gun, the fists, didn't take no sass from anybody until he got himself shot up, and where the hell he is now, nobody knows, excepting he's more than likely planted somewheres."

"Who are you talking about?"

"Nat Cullen."

Slocum didn't hesitate. He did like the cut of the

marshal's rig and he said so. "I'll square with you, J.J. I am looking for Cullen. Used to know him a while back. He wrote me, invited me to come for a look-see."

The marshal let fly again; his aim was only slightly better this time. "Young feller, you are on your own. I am telling you unofficially to get the hell out of town. I am not going to try to make you go. You ain't disturbing the peace as of this moment, and I will overlook what happened last night on account of how you helped me with young Denny, but I am telling you to ride. You have crossed Kahane and that means you have crossed Sir Archibald Tyrell and the Chelting Company. Not once— twice! With Denny Kincaid, and now beating the shit out of one of Kahane's saloons, and especially his favorite hawk, Red Weber. Slocum, you are getting mighty close to that long shadow. I am of course talking about your own."

He paused, chewing fast now, and spitting, getting some of it on his chin. "You could stay on one condition: take on as deputy."

Slocum said nothing.

"You'd be helping the law."

"Whose law?"

"That is a good question. God damn it, you know same as I do how rotten people run the rotten things and that it's all over the place. But without the law—even the times it don't work—there wouldn't be nothin'."

"I know that. And that's one reason I'm turning down your offer."

Bigelow's jaw dropped. "You got a circling way of thinking."

"Maybe. But I can find out better what I want when I am not a target. When I'm not on one side or the other."

"The law is in the middle."

"It is supposed to be. And maybe that's what you are trying. But I am right here. And when I go down it'll be for myself. That's all a man's got, Bigelow. You have the law. Good." He tapped his chest. "Slocum has got Slocum." He grinned suddenly. "Maybe it's not so different."

The marshal of Cole City shrugged.

"Got a notion where I could start looking?"

"When Cullen was sheriff he run a little business up on the North Fork of the Greybull. For sure he wouldn't be there, if he's even alive; but that ain't too far from the Kincaid Broken Hat spread, across the valley, actually. Being as you saved young Denny's neck, the boys might be glad to see you." A wicked grin suddenly appeared in his jaws, like a wolf. "Course, on the other hand, maybe they wouldn't. I dunno how they look at Cullen. And it's a tossup who drygulched him. Could be the Kincaids as easy as the Tyrell bunch."

"Is Cullen wanted?"

"You bet he is!"

"What for?"

"Running a whorehouse and taking rustled cows for payment from his customers."

Slocum didn't do much to restrain his grin at that. "Hell, a man's got to make a livin', doesn't he?"

"Not with someone else's beef."

"Maybe the boys didn't have enough money. What kind of a cathouse was it?"

"Good stuff." Then quickly, "Not that I'd know firsthand. I got me a woman."

"You're never too old," Slocum said.

The marshal spat quickly. "I might look into that."

"Did Cullen deal with merchandise that wasn't seasoned, is that what you're telling me?"

"Nope. What I understand, he dealt with quality stuff, I mean for out here, for Christ's sake!" He rolled his eyes. "But the Association said he was taking stolen stock in payment, and even running a loose iron himself."

"And he was sheriff."

"He was."

"Cute."

The marshal spat again. Then, having scored a direct hit into the spittoon, he turned in his chair, lifted his hat, and gave a wink to Alice, who was glaring at him from the counter.

Slocum took a quirly out of his shirt pocket and lit it. Then he nodded to Alice for another cup of coffee.

"Good stuff, eh?" Her grin revealed a tooth missing in the upper front and another in the lower.

"Jesus," muttered J. J. Bigelow when the girl had left. "I believe she's cottoned to you, Slocum." A gasping chuckle started in his chest, turning immediately into a cough.

"They all do," Slocum agreed pleasantly when Bigelow was again under control. "You wouldn't be hoping I'll be leading you to Cullen, would you, Marshal?"

Bigelow sniffed, cleared his throat, took a chew, and then said, "Why the hell else would I let you stay out of jail for, I mean since you wrecked the Pick-Em-Up?" He sniffed again. "Slocum, let me warn you. A lot of people could be looking for Cullen."

"Like Tyrell?"

"Like Tyrell and Kahane, and a few husbands here and there. But more serious, Tyrell and the Association could be figuring on you leading them to him."

J.J. suddenly looked cute as he cut his eye to his companion. "You know, I do hope you are aware of your friend Cullen and his sharp ways."

"Nat Cullen isn't my friend. I knew him once."

"In the War."

"Maybe."

"And you owe him one."

"Maybe."

The marshal of Cole City and environs suddenly belched. "Powerful, that coffee—if that is what it really is," he announced.

"What was you expecting, panther piss?" snapped Alice, approaching with a rag in her hand and her sleeves rolled up above her knobby elbows.

"Might taste better," Bigelow said agreeably. He reached out and patted her on the flank with his big palm.

"Keep those big paws to yerself!" She wheeled, glaring at him.

J.J. grinned all over his face. "Can't help it, you get me all horned up just walking acrost the room."

"Bullshit!"

"I am not funning!" J.J.'s grin had turned to a deeply serious expression. "I favor you."

"Go fuck yerself," muttered Alice. But they both heard it. "Or I'll be telling Lucy on you, you dirty man!" And a cackle burst from her, sounding like a chicken.

Slocum stood up, dropping money on the table. "Alice, don't let him mess with you. He is just a horny old man. I wouldn't trust him out of your sight."

"It's when he's in my sight I don't trust him, mister." And she added, "Not yourself, neither, for the matter of that." Then, blushing furiously all over her face and neck, she quickly wiped up the mess by the cuspidor, then hurried behind the counter and disappeared into the kitchen.

Chuckling, the pair left the Hello Eatery. When they were out in the street Slocum stopped and said, "Bigelow, I don't know what you heard about me. But whatever— especially what's bad—it's all true." He turned on his heel and started down the street, leaving a surprised marshal struggling with a particularly large chunk of chewing tobacco which had suddenly lodged halfway down his throat.

Save for a cut above one eyebrow, a lump on his head, bruised hands, and a sore foot where someone had tromped him, Slocum was feeling his usual good self. It was really only after parting with Bigelow outside the Hello Eatery that he took stock of himself in a physical way. The donnybrook at the Pick-Em-Up had actually made him feel pretty horny, he realized. And the action with the big blonde the night before hadn't cooled him at all. He attributed this to his physical exertion at the Pick-Em-Up.

And so when he spotted the same tall blonde with the wide shoulders driving along Main Street in the gig with the spanking black mare, passion sprang like a lion into his loins. She looked even better than she had in the San Francisco House as she sat next to the rotund man with graying hair and hands so thick his knuckles hardly showed. He had a florid face, a big nose that looked as though it had been broken more than once, and expensive-looking clothes. Her father? An uncle? Slocum couldn't imagine. When the man turned his head toward her in conversation, Slocum noted the veins in his nose, the deep pouches beneath the sharp eyes, the puffy cheeks.

Whoever it was, he looked as though he had very bad habits.

"Sir Archibald Tyrell himself in person," said the familiar voice at his elbow. He didn't have to turn around to know it was Quimby Hounds. "Or is it the beautiful young damsel who is attracting your attention, and . . . uh . . . ardor, sir?" He gave a rich chuckle. "As if I didn't know!"

Slocum smiled, not taking his eyes off the girl. At just that moment, she turned her head and looked right at him. He felt something melt all the way through him and at the same time, it was as though a flame spread from his knees right up to his throat. His smile broadened in greeting, but she simply turned away without the slightest sigh of recognition.

"Too bad," said the voice, even closer now. "Her cut is sharper than Alexander's sword, I'd say. Still, you might try for an introduction. She is, of course, Sir Archibald's."

"He must have a lot of money," Slocum said sourly.

"Indeed," said the colonel. "They're stopping at the bank. It's Tyrell's second home."

Slocum had started to walk down to where the gig had pulled up. Quimby Hounds had to step lively to keep pace with him. "Be careful, my boy. There are gunmen," he warned.

"So I see. One on the roof over there. Another at the corner of the bank alley."

"Sir Archibald always has gunmen with him. He considers himself to be quite valuable. The Box Circle has a lot of armaments."

"I guess the girl values him, too," said Slocum dryly.

"I agree with you—she's beautiful."

Slocum smiled. The colonel was cute. "Do you know her?"

"Ah, that we did. But no. We have not even touched hands, let alone anything else," the colonel said in his royal tone. "We have not had the pleasure of even a small smile." He spread his pale hands, shrugging. "We simply don't exist for such people."

While they stood watching, Sir Archibald got down. Still holding the reins of the shiny black mare in one hand, he offered his other hand to the girl. Together they walked to the door of the bank, which had opened to allow an erect middle-aged man dressed in gray to stand framed in the doorway. His voice carried so that Slocum and the colonel could hear him.

"Ah, Sir Archibald. How good of you to come. What a surprise. And . . ." He did not finish his sentence but, bowing to the girl, his lips brushed the hand she offered.

"Swanky, wot, old boy?" said the colonel, laying on a British accent, but so only Slocum might hear.

When the bank door closed behind the trio, the colonel said, "I take it that you thought you knew her."

"We did run into each other."

"But she cut you."

"You're very observant," Slocum said with a touch of vinegar.

The colonel suddenly whipped out his bright red bandanna and wiped his nose, his mouth, and then his eyes. He had been leaning lightly on his malacca cane, but such was the vigor of his wiping that he almost lost his balance. All at once he blew his nose loudly. He sneezed, then he coughed. Finally he belched, and released an enormous sigh.

"Liquid support is clearly called for, Slocum. I suggest

the Can't Lose Saloon and Gaming Hall as appropriate to the occasion."

Slocum squinted at the sun. He was planning on riding out to the Kincaid place, but there was time. And he wanted to visit young Denny first.

Seated at a corner in the Can't Lose, the colonel offered his companion a fresh havana, then struck a lucifer and both lighted up.

"The finest," Quimby Hounds murmured, his words ponderous with sanctimony.

Both leaned back in their chairs, enjoying the cigars in which Colonel Quimby Hounds took such pride and delight.

Now, reaching into a coat pocket, he withdrew some brown wrapping paper and opened it. Slocum immediately remembered the copy of the newspaper Hounds had brought him and which he hadn't read.

"You're printing on that kind of paper?" he exclaimed in surprise.

"We are often short of paper, my boy, so we are forced to accept a—shall we say—a strategic retreat. Now, before you get to whatever you wish to speak about, hear this. Fresh off the press. A bit of local color, the temper and tone of Cole City. I believe you will appreciate it!"

The colonel was smiling as he read, "When the Reverend Cletus Feerwelling walked into the Happy Times Saloon this past Thursday at precisely nine o'clock on a supposedly quiet evening, his ears met the crash of pistol fire. Two drovers from the Quarter and Cutbank outfit down at Big Butte were having an altercation over cards. Sloshed with trade whiskey and unable to hit the side of the proverbial barn, their firing had in consequence swept the entire clientele to the floor.

"Even the reverend, a man of God, took cover, not completely certain, perhaps, that the Lord covers the world of saloons and other sporty establishments," he added with a wet chuckle to Slocum.

"I'll hear about this, Slocum," he went on in a further aside. And he continued reading. "Rufus Thistle was wounded in the right arm. His opponent in the engagement, a gentleman passing through who gave the name McNab Boles, was hit in the hand. However, the shooting was at such close range and the powder so thick that witnesses—not only befogged because of the gunsmoke, but as a result of the liquor—were not at all together in their descriptions of the passage at arms. It is claimed that Burt Wilfong, one of the cardplayers who received much lead in his arms, legs, and chest, indeed would be dead now had he not been so inebriated at the time. Reliable sources maintain that Doc Mohun has urged Burt's friends to keep him well tanked with alcohol for fear that if the gentleman ever sobers up he will indeed kick the bucket."

Whereupon the colonel dissolved, almost driven to the floor with mirth.

It was just at this moment that Slocum heard the drumbeat of horses pounding down the street, accompanied by the brisk sound of gunfire.

The colonel pushed back his chair, but before he could get to his feet a bald-headed man with a limp burst into the saloon.

"It's the Kincaids! They got Denny!"

"Sit down," Slocum said to the colonel. "Finish your drink."

The colonel sank into his chair and reached for his glass. "Good thinking, Slocum. They didn't waste any time."

"They picked the best time," Slocum said. "Towns are always sleepy at noon."

5

Just at midnight the storm started with a sudden driving wind from the northwest, thrashing the land with sleet. It was late in spring for that kind of weather, but that didn't stop it. It kept on until almost morning, when the wind slackened and the sleet turned to a cold, drizzling rain, soaking everything.

In the pre-dawn it stopped, and the sky cleared as the sun's rays shot up behind the horizon, throwing golden light into the morning sky. In a short while the land welcomed it, emitting little plumes of steam as the warmth met the cold and wet left by the passing storm.

In the round horse corral, steam rose from the soaking withers and backs of the horses. There were six of these and they stood in two groups of three huddled close to the corral poles, waiting the way horses do.

In the cabin three of the Kincaids were seated with the fourth, their young brother Denny. All were drinking coffee; the three older brothers had built cigarettes and were smoking.

"An' so he shot the rope, did he!" Boone Kincaid, the eldest, at twenty-five, repeated the news Denny had brought. Boone was the biggest, with a strong body and quick temper.

The boy nodded. "Th-th-that's wh-what he d-d-done."

"Pretty good shooting," Boone said, his words soft with a reluctant admiration.

"And then?" Kelly, the next oldest, asked.

"Th-then I-I b-b-blacked out."

"Jesus..." It was an ejaculation of awe rather than of anger or alarm which came from Boone, the accepted head of the family.

"Who is this un?" asked Ives, who had just turned twenty-two. He had a long, thin face and a scraggly beard. Shorter than his three brothers, he was nevertheless wider than all of them except Boone, thus giving the impression of being as wide as he was high, which had been a joke in the family and with neighbors most of his life.

"Heard his name was Slocum," Kelly Kincaid said. "Ever hear of him, Boone?"

"No, I never." Boone flexed his fingers, then took the cigarette out of his mouth, emitting a cloud of smoke that rose to the ceiling of the cabin. Boone was known to be swift as a striking snake with that big gun at his hip.

Ives turned to his kid brother. "Denny, who is this feller? He a lawman?"

"D-d-dunno."

"But he was with Bigelow," Kelly said.

"He-he w-w-was on the st-stage."

"That's what we heard," Boone said. "That don't tell us nothing."

"Shit, Boone, what we gonna do now?" Ives asked. "They'll be coming after." He looked at Denny, who was still eating.

Boone hitched at his trousers as he stood up. "We will do what Paw always told us to do," he said, and he nodded to emphasize those words.

"What's that?" Kelly asked the question, and both he and Ives watched their older brother for an answer.

"Shit, you remember! He said, 'What'll you do when it rains—shit, you let it rain!'"

All four of them burst into a great roar of laughter. It was just what was needed to break the fog that had been enveloping them.

"Good enough," Boone said as they subsided. "They will come after Denny, and we will be waiting. It is time for us to face the bastards."

"You don't think it'd be smarter to pull up into the mountains, Boone?" Kelly asked.

"If I'd thought that I'd of said it."

Kelly's face twisted. He didn't like it. "I was just saying that I think..."

"Stop thinking," his brother told him. "It'll rot yer brain."

At this Ives let out a hoot, and Denny grinned, life suddenly coming back into his eyes.

"Fuck you," Kelly said, and with a belch followed by a nod of his head, he picked up his coffee.

Boone said nothing. He was used to the upstart ways of his kid brother—number two itching to be number one. He didn't take it seriously, nor did Kelly.

They were a close bunch, the Kincaids. Paw had made it so, and Maw even more. When both parents had died in the cattle stampede the feisty boys had drawn even

69

tighter together. As Paw lay dying, not knowing—for
they'd agreed not to tell him—that his Lily had been
killed in the stampede; he had told them to take care of
her and Denny. And then, asking for her, wanting to see
her, his eyes had suddenly gone blank. And he had almost
finished his dying when the thought of Lily had brought
a smile to his face. All of them remembered that, Abel
Kincaid smiling at his beloved Lily as he met her in
another world, both of them dead from the stampede.

Such a scene did in no way mitigate their rage at the
Chelting Land and Cattle Company, whose steers had
done the deed. Relations with the big stockgrowers had
been brittle for some time, but Paw had kept it cool, Paw
leading the smaller stockmen. Now it was Boone, Boone
and his brothers, who had rallied the whole valley in
revenge.

"Who c-c-coming after?" the boy asked now.

"The fucking law, that's who," Kelly said.

"And the Box Circle," Ives added.

"Same thing," Kelly said.

"Not the same," Boone put in now. "Not the same.
Bigelow is his own man."

"Kahane and them can wipe him out right now," Kelly
said, his tone surly.

"That's a gut all right," his older brother conceded.
"And for sure, if Bigelow did have Denny back in that
jail, those lynching sons of bitches would be busting in."

"Like they done at Junction with the lot of us," Ives
said. "Denny, how's yer neck?" he asked, suddenly turning to his brother, taking the heat away from Boone and
Kelly. Ives had always been the mediator. It had been
Ives who had taken most care of Denny ever since he'd
been tromped by the big sorrel stallion.

"All-all right."

"You hurtin'?"

"Only when I-I g-g-got throwed. My ass."

All of them laughed at that, save Boone. The older Kincaid was standing at one of the portholes peering out, and they had hardly noticed when he'd gotten up and walked away from the table.

Now Kelly said, "What you see, Boone?"

Boone turned back. "Throw me them," he said, nodding to the glasses on a shelf by the jumbo stove.

"What you see?" Kelly asked again.

His brother spoke with his eyes still peering through the lenses. "It is fairing off." And he turned back to face the others. His cigarette was out, the paper and a few shreds of tobacco hanging on his lower lip. He spat it onto the dirt floor as he reached to the pocket of his hickory shirt for the makings.

Ives picked up the coffee pot and began pouring. Kelly started to pick his teeth with the end of a wooden match which he had whittled to a point with his Bowie knife. For several moments they were silent, each turning over the desperate situation in which they found themselves, between the law on one side, and the big Stockgrowers' Association led by Archibald Tyrell and his Box Circle spread on the other.

"Fuck 'em," muttered Boone.

His brothers murmured in agreement.

The Broken Hat spread, born from the hand of Abel Kincaid and his wife and four sons, lay high up under the rimrocks of Jeffry Mountain, part of the range of the Absarokas. The cabin was uniquely placed. Almost invisible to anyone approaching, it afforded a clear view of the trail all the way down to the river, with two exceptions where it wound through willows and cotton-woods in twice crossing the creek that ribboned down the side of the mountain.

The cabin itself was a fortress. Built of spruce logs, its thick walls could resist the most determined bullets. There were portholes, besides the windows, through which to fire at unwelcome visitors. Abel Kincaid had thought of everything, which indeed was only the basic require-ment for a life such as his and his family's.

For, like so many men of that time and place, Abel had built his herd by branding mavericks with his Broken Hat brand. Others did the same, but when the Chelting Company came on the scene Archibald Tyrell and several other big cattlemen of the western Wyoming country viewed such procedures as unfavorable to the growth of their own herds, and so condemned the practice as illegal. The fact that most of them had started their own herds in similar fashion was considered of no consequence to the big owners. Those were the old days; and this here was now. The small cattlemen, the group named by the Association as maverickers, saw differently. Branding unmothered slicks went on. Since the beginning, un-branded stock had been considered bounty for anyone who put his iron on it.

When Swede Greenough, Tyrell's range foreman, found cattle with changed brands he claimed had been Box Circle but had now been altered with a running iron to three other outfits, Sir Archibald Tyrell decided it was time to act. The problem was getting very much worse. Realizing that the Kincaids were the driving force amongst the maverickers, Sir Archibald moved swiftly. It was a simple plan. Five witnesses swore that the Kincaid broth-ers had set fire to the Box Circle line camp up on Wood

Creek, and had at the same time shot at two cowmen in the process. Attempted murder and arson on top of rustling! An irate twenty-man posse led by Red Weber caught up with the brothers at a time when they had no idea of what had happened—indeed, they had been miles away from the action—and clapped them into the Junction Crossing jail. A lynching had been averted only by the intervention of Sheriff Nat Cullen. But later a mob led by Kahane had attacked the jail with the result that the Kincaids took advantage of the moment to make a break for it, unfortunately losing Denny when he was thrown from his horse. In the process Sheriff Cullen, only just beginning to recover from wounds inflicted by Clyde Allnut, had been gunned almost down to his pockets by a drygulcher who shot at him with a goosegun when he was just leaving the outhouse behind the sheriff's office.

"You rested?" Ives asked Denny.

"M-m-my l-legs hu-hurt."

"Shit, we had to tie you to the mare. Figured you wouldn't stay on otherwise."

"You feel all right, Denny?" Kelly asked. "How's yer neck?"

"All right."

The boy's lips were wet. He was eating quickly, using his spoon some of the time, and then picking up the hominy grits and venison with his fingers and shoving it into his mouth. Bent over his tin plate, his eyes stared at nothing.

"We'll get Kahane for this," Boone promised, turning back from the porthole. His eyes slipped to the log walls. They were thick, some as much as ten inches in diameter, chinked with strips of wood on the inside and mud and manure on the outside.

"Bigelow will be after him for this," Kelly said, nodding toward Denny.

"After Denny, you mean, or Kahane?" said Ives.

"Both. Bigelow won't let Kahane get away with that is what I am saying."

"Bigelow won't be able to do much when he is deader'n hell," observed Boone.

"B-Ba-Barney Tr-Traherne, he-he tr-tried t-t-t-to g-get 'em to wa-wa-wait."

"Didn't do much good, did he?" said Ives sardonically. He looked at each of his brothers. "You think he needs Doc?"

"How's your neck?" Boone asked.

Denny tried to move his head and winced painfully.

"Reckon you'd be dead now if it wasn't for that feller on the stage," Ives said.

"Jesus!" grunted Boone.

"Denny is hurtin'," Ives said in defense.

Boone had turned back to the porthole and was peering through the glasses.

"What you see, Boone?"

"See some customers over to Millicent's place."

"Yeah?" Kelly came to stand beside him. "How many?"

"Three horses in the corral."

"That gal's gonna wear it out," said Ives with a laugh.

"You never wear it out, boy," Boone said, still looking through the glasses at the cabin across the valley on the east side of the river.

Ives looked at his brother Denny. "He looks like he's been stomped and dragged; needs some sleep."

"Think he needs Doc?" Kelly asked.

"More likely he needs some of Miss Millicent," Boone

said, still with his back to the room. Suddenly he turned and faced them. "By God, that is just what I need."

At the livery barn Slocum decided to give the spotted pony a rest, so he rented a blue roan with a thin white blaze on his forehead. He was a chunky horse with one white stocking and a mean cast in his left eye. Slocum got the message when he was cinching the saddle and the beast turned his head back to look at him out of that crazy eye. The next minute he had snapped his big teeth at Slocum's arm.

"Stop that, you buggery bastard!" He slapped the animal right on the nose. Blue was his color and it was his name too; and he didn't like that slap on his nose. But his rider, he soon saw, was a man of no nonsense.

Slocum led him out of the livery and swung up into his old stock saddle. Blue tried to drop his head and spin, but Slocum was too fast for him. With a firm grip on the reins he kept the horse's head up and gave him a couple of sharp licks across the rump.

"Told you he could get ornery," the old hostler said.

"I am not arguing it," Slocum replied. "I want something with some spirit, not some old crowbait."

"That's what the man said when he went to the cathouse," grumbled the old hostler, who had a patch over one eye. He was an old man who looked as though caved in. Slocum figured him for an old bronc stomper; or maybe something else had busted him up. When the roan had settled some, he sat there in the saddle looking down at the hostler.

"I am heading south," he said. "Know the next town, do you?"

"South, eh?" The hostler spat through his gray-yellow mustache, getting some of the spittle on his shirt, though not noticing, and maybe not even caring, Slocum could see. "Next outfit you'll run into if you take the crossing down by Split Butte'll be the Logan place." He sniffed, then lifted his eye patch and scratched into the deep red eyeless socket. "South?" he repeated. "Figured you might be headin' out to Kincaids'." And he put the patch back over his eye.

"Don't figure so much, old-timer—you'll live longer." And with a wicked grin Slocum turned the roan and started out of town heading south.

It was early. The first sunlight was washing over the wooden town. As he rode out a cock crowed; he heard a dog bark. Crossing the creek just below Cole City, the roan started to crowhop, spooked by something or other, but again Slocum cut him a couple of good licks, and that settled it. When he was well out of sight of the town he began to circle so that by the middle of the forenoon he was headed north toward the Kincaids' Broken Hat.

He kept the roan at a walk now, moving past good, lush bunch grass and a couple of buffalo wallows, with his eyes returning again and again to those great snow-capped peaks that thrust right into the azure sky and never seemed to get any closer.

As he rode, the things he saw and smelled—a bunch of deer feeding near a cutbank, the low tableland down past Horse Creek, the rich smell of the roan, the tang of the crackling day—all touched something in him that he needed.

It was often like that, that touch, the feel of his life running through his body; a streaming, tingling, yes—like sexual pleasure, but not only in the loins—it went all through him, a glowing that he had known as a boy, when the days were never long enough; and, too, like the wondrous nights when sometimes he'd awaken and lie in his bed unable to wait for morning to come.

Around mid-afternoon he reached the old wooden bridge that crossed the river and met the trail which he had been told would lead him to the Kincaid place, the highest outfit in the country. It was a wooden bridge built of logs and limbs and supported by triangular log pilings that were filled with rocks. The whole shebang was tied by ropes to trees along the river banks. He wondered how the bridge would handle a spring breakup with its chunks of ice and globs of snow and other debris racing through. It didn't look too safe even now, and he could feel the strain on those ropes, for the river was still fairly full, though not over its banks.

Turning the roan he walked him into a shallow place along the river bank and let him drink while the water washed over his legs and refreshed them. Meanwhile, he let his eyes search upward toward the Kincaid spread, which was not visible. He knew roughly where to look just below the high rimrocks. Old man Kincaid had picked well, he could see. The kind of place a man couldn't spot till he was right on top of it.

Slocum touched his heels to the roan's belly and rode out of the water and up onto the rickety bridge. It was shaky going. About halfway over Blue spooked at something and almost lost his footing. Slocum thought for a second they were going over, but the animal regained himself.

Now the sun was hot on his hands as they started up the long, winding trail on the other side of the river.

He had no notion of what he was going to do or even

say when he got to the Kincaid spread. For all he knew they might start shooting at him; for surely they could see anyone approaching and—if they so wished—pick them off. But he had figured boldness was the best way. After all, he had saved young Kincaid from a lynching. And no doubt Denny was up there now with them. It was no guarantee, however, of safe passage. In times of cattle wars and lynching, tempers were short and trigger fingers nervous. Clearly the situation was past the talk stage and into the action. But the Kincaids were his lead to Nat Cullen. It could even be that Cullen was up there right now.

And Cullen could be dead right now, what was more. The colonel had laid it on thick. "He is likely more dead than alive right now," Quimby Hounds had put it. "He might not make it. He just might not!" He had looked down at his pale hands then. "I cottoned to Cullen. A good man. But like all the Dutch—and I am one, sir— there are moments when his head is thick."

"How do you mean that?" Slocum had asked with a grin.

"Nat . . . uh . . . tarried a little longer here in Cole City, not so much because of his business enterprise—unique though it was, and very likely still is—but on account of a young lady, and I do mean young, and good-looking too by any standards, whom he bedded, evidently with great zeal and vigor, not to mention frequency."

Slocum had chuckled at that. "People never change, do they?"

"If they ever do, it's inevitably for the worse," the colonel had replied dourly. "However, the young lady was married."

"But of course! Cullen wouldn't have gotten himself

into something easy and simple!"

"Married to Mr. Red Weber."

"Jesus!"

"Indeed, it is the moment to invoke the deity; and as we know you have met the gentleman, the husband in question." The colonel had looked down at Slocum's bruised and raw knuckles as he continued. "Things came to the boil when Nat braced Weber and the big man backwatered. Nobody would believe it. Nat is no muscle man, as you well know. But, by the Almighty, he is all guts! He cut Weber right off at his shoes. The short of it was that Nat stayed on and took the sheriff's job. And not only that—and here is the fly in the ointment, my friend—he made his way into a successful though highly volatile business operation up on the North Fork, just across from the Kincaids."

"Are you saying he was running a cathouse out in the mountains?"

"Unique, eh? One thinks of such enterprises being run in town. But Nat, as anyone can see, had an original way of doing things."

"And . . . what, he refused to pay off Kahane?"

"You have brought the story right up to date, sir!"

Slocum grinned, thinking of the colonel as he rode up toward the Broken Hat. But what about Tyrell and his big English company? It rankled people in the country having those dudes come in and run things, when they none of them knew their ass from a buffalo chip. Of course they carried the money. But the dudes were ruining the West. So said any self-respecting cattleman. And especially the small outfits; especially the mavericks. True, some of the big men were all right, but men like Tyrell with their gunmen and ramrods like Weber and

Kahane . . . he could see how Cullen had inevitably run afoul of that breed.

And then, the girl Rhonda! It was as though she had simply disappeared. He wondered whether he would ever see her again.

At that moment he saw a jackrabbit break for cover, and his eyes came to pinpoints as he drew rein next to a large boulder. Nothing. Nothing was moving anywhere. What was it, then? Suddenly he swung clean around in his saddle to look at his back trail. He was out of sight of the Broken Hat, he figured, protected from above by a shield of box elders. Even so, the Kincaids could have outriders posted. What then? Why did he have that sudden so-familiar sense of danger?

The roan had lifted his head and was listening. Slocum watched his ears. Only the call of a jay in the heated afternoon. The roan's ears went forward, to the side, then forward again. Slocum reached to his waist and undid the leather thong holding his Colt.

"Don't draw it!"

The voice was hard, and the three men who rode from the stand of box elders had their guns in their hands. He did not recognize any of them, neither from the lynching nor from Cole City.

Slocum had let his hand fall away from his sixgun.

"You want something, mister? This here is Broken Hat range." The speaker was a man with a long chest and thin arms.

"I'm looking for the Kincaids."

"What you want with the Kincaids?" a man in tight clothing demanded. "State your business."

But before he could answer, the third man spoke; he was wearing a blue bandanna around his head. "Boone, he looks to me like one of Tyrell's men."

"Are you Boone Kincaid?" Slocum asked. "I know your brother Denny. He'll speak for me. Where is he?"

The moment that followed was only a beat too long, and he knew that feeling again; something was definitely wrong.

"Where is Denny?" he said again. "He knows me."

"Denny's still in the jailhouse, for Christ's sake," said the man with the long chest, and his long fingers moved idly on his sixgun.

In that split second of the other man's loss of attention, Slocum threw himself off the roan toward the big boulder, drawing his Colt as he did so. Landing on his left shoulder, he rolled, as the bullets cracked around him, and he fired at the riders whose horses were rearing, pulling up behind the big rock by the side of the trail, miraculously not hit. He could hear them cursing as they scattered into the box elders. Suddenly he saw something move and he fired. Someone screamed out an oath. Then it was silent.

Who were they? Pretending to be Kincaids to throw him off guard! His quick move had caught them by surprise, for they hadn't known Denny Kincaid was no longer in jail. He was watching the box elders for any movement, listening for the least sound, and he also had his attention on the blue roan, who was standing only a few yards from him. When he saw the roan lift his head with his ears twitching, he knew. At the precise moment that he rolled, the gunshot sounded like thunder in his ear. Something hit him from behind. And somewhere he heard a man shouting, "God damn it, where the fuck were you? We set him up! Where the fuck was you?" It was like a dream, but he was sure it was Red Weber's voice shouting that they'd better get out before the Kincaids came.

And then there were more shouts. He heard the drumming of horses' hooves.

Someone was leaning over him.

"It's-it's S-Slo-Slocum."

There were four of them there in the dimming light; two were off their horses, while the other two remained mounted. He could smell the whiskey lacing the sweet mountain air as the sun settled down on the far rimrocks across the wide valley. He heard the roan nicker nearby.

"Wh-what hap-happened?" Denny asked.

He felt slowly over his head, not making any fast moves. One of the men had knelt beside him and was looking at his head.

"You got nicked. Close but no cigar."

"He all-all r-r-right, B-B-Boone?" asked Denny.

"He's nicked."

Slocum had started to sit up now.

"It-it w-w-was h-h-him s-s-saved me," said Denny.

"Slocum, huh," Boone said.

"I was . . . I reckon I still am." He sat all the way up now, rubbing the back of his neck. Someone's hand came forward with his hat.

"What happened?" asked Kelly from his horse.

Slocum squinted up at the two riders. "You the Kincaids?"

"All four of us," Ives said.

"There were three of them set me up pretending to be Kincaids and they had a fourth ready to backshoot me. Luckily his timing was off."

"Who were they?"

"Dunno." His head ached and he wanted to vomit.

"Likely Red Weber's men," Boone said. "We heard of you whipping that son of a bitch and wrecking the whole of the Pick-Em-Up. Ten will get you twenty it was them; his men, anyways."

Slocum rose slowly to his feet. Once up, he felt better, but he wanted to be sure and not make any fast moves that might be trouble.

"This yourn?" Boone handed him his gun. "Well, you ain't dead, and you ain't in hell nor heaven."

"It'll be Tyrell's men," one of the horsemen said.

"That is what was just said," Boone said. "Why in hell don't you listen one time, Kelly?"

Kelly belched suddenly and said, "I could use another drink."

Denny Kincaid pushed close to Slocum now. "We-we h-h-heard the sh-sh-shootin'."

"Four of 'em," said Ives softly to nobody in particular.

"C'mon to the house," Kelly said. "Give you drink and some grub."

"W-we heard the sh-sh-shootin' all the w-way to-to-to M-M-Mi..."

"Millicent's," Ives said, filling in impatiently.

"Shut up!" snapped Boone. "Don't have to tell everybody in the whole entire country our business, you dumb shit!"

"I only—"

But his brother's booming voice cut him right off. "He might of helped Denny here, and we 'preciate that, but he is still not known to us. We do not know who the hell he is, and what he is doing up here on Broken Hat range. Say, what you doing up here anyways, mister?"

"I am looking for Nat Cullen."

Denny started to open his mouth, but Boone was quicker.

"Never heard of him," Boone said.

"Cullen is a friend of mine. I've got a letter. I'm sure you've heard of Sheriff Nat Cullen."

"Well, why didn't you say so?"

"I am saying so now, mister. If you know where he is, then I'd like you to tell me." He looked hard at the chunky Boone Kincaid, who was standing there in the trail as though rooted.

"What's yer name?" Boone asked.

"B-B-Boone, I-I-I t-t-to-told . . ."

"Shut up!" his brother snapped. "He can tell me his name."

But Slocum had already dropped his gunbelt and now took a step toward the other man. He pointed at Boone's waist. "You drop your gun, sonny, and I'll teach you some manners."

Boone didn't go through the formality of unbuckling his gunbelt, but simply charged. Slocum had gauged him correctly. Sidestepping, he put out his foot and Boone tripped over it. As he started to fall, Slocum brought a wicked left around and smashed him on the side of the jaw. The oldest Kincaid fell like a log, dead to the world.

"Anybody else?" Slocum, with his eyes still on the remaining Kincaids, reached down and retrieved his gunbelt.

"Jesus . . . !" muttered Kelly Kincaid.

"Now you gentlemen can tell me where to find Nat Cullen. Would he be up at your outfit?" He jerked his thumb over his shoulder. "Or . . ." He finished buckling his gunbelt. "Over at—who was it, Millicent's?"

They were speechless.

Slocum waited. The figure at his feet had begun to stir, and Slocum undid the hammer thong on his Colt, just in case. He waited while Boone Kincaid rose unsteadily and stood facing him. There was a silly grin on his face.

"I do reckon you are a friend of Nat's," he said. "Nobody else could've had that kind of balls."

Slocum felt a grin moving over his face. Boone was all right. He was genuine.

"Nat is over to Millicent's," Boone said. "But it ain't doing him any good. He's about done for. He is dyin' for sure, if not already dead."

"I can't think of a better place to cash in than a cathouse," Slocum said.

"We'll get us some grub up to the house. Then you can go see Nat," Boone said, rubbing his jaw. "I owe you one, by God. I'll just have to find the right excuse."

6

The brick building was unique for that part of the country. It surely dominated the Box Circle spread, and much else. Two stories high, with a verandah on one side. The appointments inside this mansion were of the best quality: furnishings, silverware, crockery, glasses, pictures, and decorations, whatever the eye rested upon had been sent from San Francisco, Denver, Chicago, or the East, and much of it from "home," home being England. Sir Archibald Tyrell believed in living well, and he was a man who carried out his belief in action.

He sat now at the head of the large table, looking down at the faces of the men on either side. There were four besides himself, and they had spent an enjoyable time working their way from soup to dessert and coffee. All of which had been accompanied by good liquor and wine and amiable conversation.

"Collins." Sir Archibald, florid-faced, corpulent, looking rather like John Bull, that symbol of British acquisitiveness and tenacity, spoke with the gentleness of unlimited power to his butler. Collins had also been brought from "home" along with much of Sir Archibald's necessaries, including his favorite decanters, his fox-hunting prints, guns, and shooting cups and other trophies.

"Yes, Sir Archibald?"

"Cigars all round."

"Yes, Sir Archibald."

The talk at luncheon had been casual with now and again a well-placed anecdote to keep things going. Sir Archibald was a master at whetting the emotional appetites of those with whom he dealt. He knew how to take his time. By the end of the meal everyone was keyed to whatever their host had to say; in a word, receptive.

These were members of the Stockgrowers' Association, four of the more important men, at least as far as Sir Archibald was concerned. They ran the biggest spreads in that part of the country, and hence were most directly affected by the situation regarding rustling. Sir Archibald didn't believe in working in large numbers, and like any sensible politician he dealt with individuals, key people; his principle being more the lever than the numerical vote. And as he sat back now in his comfortable chair he was reflecting on how he did hold the keys to the present thorny affair.

For these were concerned men. They had not risen to their present station by being easygoing, careless, or in any way hampered by such sentiments as remorse or pity. They were the kind who had inherited only what they had fought for.

They had suffered that terrible winter not long past when the herds had frozen and the prairie had turned into a sheet of ice all the way from Texas to Montana, when neither cow nor steer was able to paw through snow and ice for feed. The animals had starved, dying ganted and too weak to stand; during the spring breakup the rivers had swelled with the corpses of rotting cattle, while the land was dotted with endless carcasses. In Wyoming alone the overall loss had been put at fifty percent.

They would never forget it. Never. And the memory of it would pass through generations to come. Now another threat was at hand. And it wasn't the weather; it was men. But men they knew how to deal with. This time they would not be beaten. Archibald Tyrell had said so, and so had his four guests: Clarence Fahnstock, Clyde Bowdoin, Miles Calmer, and Bill Fanting.

"I thought it made sense," Sir Archibald was saying, "to have a meeting with just a few of us rather than the whole of the Association, which we can do down in Cheyenne later if necessary. The point being to see our way clear on this situation which has suddenly become . . . uh . . . a bit knotty." He dropped a little laugh and the company responded by loosening themselves even more.

"Good enough." Clarence Fahnstock nodded. He was a tall, weathered man who had brought his herds up from Texas and had fought the Kiowa and Comanche in his time. Fahnstock had a long nose, down which he generally surveyed men such as Sir Archibald, dudes who had come out from England with a greedy purse and no love for the country, yet with plenty of business savvy. Which, Fahnstock had to admit, was needed. Since that frightful winter English money was as good as gold, or even blood. They all needed it. So they put up with the damn dudes like Tyrell and Fanting.

Sir Archibald knew exactly how Fahnstock and some of the others felt about the English, and especially himself. It didn't bother him at all. People were for use; he didn't give a bloody damn what they thought inside their fat heads.

"We are one reasonably small corner of the great American West," he was now saying, "but an important corner. What happens here in western Wyoming will surely affect the whole cattle situation. I am, of course, speaking of the increase in rustling and lawlessness."

He paused, his thick fingers and thumb touching the polished glass into which Collins had just poured brandy.

"We're heading into a real tight, if that's what you mean," Miles Calmer said. He ran the palm of his hand over his high, slightly damp forehead. Calmer was a small, knotty man with a Scottish accent, who looked as though he lived in a holster and could get off a shot at any moment.

Sir Archibald accepted a cigar from the box Collins was offering. "What is happening here is similar to what is happening all over; and, of course, if unchecked, it will increase a hundred fold." As he spoke he was punching a little hole in the end of his cigar, having first pressed it between his thumb and fingers and sniffed it for freshness. Now he bent his head for the light Collins offered. "And the manner in which we—we five here at this table—deal with the situation will set the tone, the pattern for the rest. We must—and we will—stop it at its very roots, I am saying."

"By God, I follow that!" Clyde Bowdoin, a man with a lot of black hair sprouting out of his nose and ears, brought the palm of his hand down flat on the table in emphasis. From behind him Collins's eyes flew upward in vast disapproval as some of the silverware clattered in protest.

Sir Archibald, catching his butler's reaction, smiled covertly.

"But what are we going to do about their early roundup?" Clyde Bowdoin said. He was a man with very pale eyes. Sometimes a person looked into them and felt lost, even frightened. It was said that Bowdoin had killed a lot of men. He no longer carried a gun. Some men didn't need to. He was sixty or thereabouts, with very big wrist bones, giving some people the impression that his wrists had been broken.

"You're speaking of the Kincaids' plan for an early gather so the maverickers get their brands on before the rest of us," Sir Archibald said.

Bowdoin nodded.

Clarence Fahnstock put down his empty brandy glass. "It'll be a whole month early; too early for us to move on it," he said, and his lips were grim. Fahnstock was a man who liked to move fast, like Bowdoin and Calmer. He had small patience with men like Bill Fanting, who always wanted to take time to study a situation and talk it over. Yet he was not impulsive to the point of recklessness. Fahnstock ran a big herd just north of the Flint River.

"And you realize it will not be, so to say, legal, what they're doing," Fanting, of the Anglo–American Cattle & Beef Corporation, said. He spoke with the clipped English of a Liverpool man, from whence he in fact hailed. Sir Archibald considered his fellow countryman small beer, to use his own expression, but he respected the man's zeal for money and his insensitivity to other people's pain.

"But what are we going to do about it?" Miles Calmer exclaimed. "If we let them get away with that, then they'll just think they can get away with anything." He coughed suddenly, his throat rattling. "You realize—we all must realize—that to allow it is to invite ruin!" He had spoken leaning forward with one arm on the white tablecloth, and now he sat back, opening his knobby hands in an offering gesture, while the lines in his forehead rose, some of them almost disappearing as he nodded his hard head in emphasis of what he had just said. "You know," he resumed. "You know I am concerned. Something has got to be done!" He leaned forward again to sweep the glass of brandy into his hand. Raising it in a swift, wordless toast, he drank vigorously. Gasping, he put the empty glass down, after which he patted his chest.

Now it was Fahnstock who, holding his unlighted cigar between his thumb and forefinger, used it as a pointer to review. "We've had our stock stolen right and left. There has been fighting, and there's been two killings." He shrugged, throwing one long hand toward the ceiling to emphasize the situation. "The man—or the men—at the bottom of it are, as we know, the Kincaids. Boone Kincaid is the leader and they've roused the whole of the valley and Coyote Basin as well to side with 'em!"

"Then kill him. Kill them, kill the Kincaids." The words fell softly into the pause that followed Fahnstock's hard words. Sir Archibald added, "After all, he—*they*— are breaking the law."

"We have again and again warned them," Bowdoin pointed out, "and we've had them in jail. Matt Kahane tried to hang one of them." He threw up his hands. "It seems to me we have to take direct action ourselves."

"Precisely," said Sir Archibald. "That is precisely what

I suggest. Do listen." He paused, eyeing them carefully in turn. "The hanging of one of the Kincaids I understand was aborted by this man . . . what's his name?" He snapped his fingers, looking around for the name.

"Slocum," Calmer said. "John Slocum."

"Who is he?" He waved a hand. "I've heard of him, of course—how he wrecked one of the saloons in town; but tell me what you know."

There was a pause as some of the men looked at each other. Finally, Clarence Fahnstock spoke. "I have heard of Slocum. He is a tough one."

"A law officer?" Sir Archibald asked.

"Oh, no." Something like a pained smile touched Fahnstock's face. "Not that."

"Is he a road agent, you're saying?" Miles Calmer asked.

Fahnstock shook his head. "He's his own man. I've heard he rode with Quantrill." He waited, while all felt the change in the atmosphere.

"Is this Slocum man working with the Kincaids?" Bill Fanting asked.

"I believe he was simply on the stage when Kahane and his men stopped it and took the young Kincaid. Why he rescued him isn't clear." Fahnstock leaned back in his chair and looked along his arm to the glass he was holding on the table. It was empty.

"I understand Cullen is dead," Sir Archibald said suddenly.

"It is believed so." Bill Fanting shrugged.

"But not sure."

"No one has actually seen the corpse," Fanting said. "But from the way he was described to me, he would be better off dead. Kahane's men didn't mess that one."

"Like they did the hanging," put in Clyde Bowdoin sourly.

"We must be careful, and not go too far," Sir Archibald cautioned.

"But didn't you just say to kill the Kincaids?" Miles Calmer's Scots accent was as thick as a thorn patch, and he could hardly get the words out.

A smile touched Sir Archibald's lips. "Yes, that is so. But it was not shouted from the housetops. It was said softly, carefully." He paused, watching them, gauging where they were. He knew he had them slightly confused; that was what he wanted. He let a little sigh push past his lips. "It is the time for being clever. Brute force has failed. The maverickers depend on the Kincaids, especially on Boone. Get rid of them and we've broken the rustlers."

"Agreed," said Fanting, nodding his head.

Sir Archibald Tyrell looked coldly at him. "Bigelow is our problem," he said.

"Bigelow!" Fahnstock threw his head around to stare at their host.

"Bigelow is the law. He is an appointed officer of the law, not elected, the way Cullen was, and so not political in that sense. Moreover, I have heard from many quarters that J. J. Bigelow really *is* the law; he takes his job seriously."

"He surely does." Clyde Bowdoin sighed.

"All of which is to our advantage." A smile broadened on Sir Archibald's face. "We are law-abiding men, and so we will have nothing to do with violence, with guns and killing. That is for others. Otherwise, we will alienate Bigelow and turn the valley against us. What I am saying—" He held up his hand to stem any possible objection from the others. "What I am saying is that we have to look right with the law. And so we will do nothing overt. For we do not want trouble with the authorities."

Again Sir Archibald paused, while his eyes moved slowly around the group at the table.

"I never met an authority yet who couldn't be bought," laughed Bill Fanting.

"You can't buy J. J. Bigelow, Bill." Fahnstock cocked a cold eye at his colleague as he spoke. "Not that I don't wish we could," he added.

"Except Bigelow," Fanting amended with a little laugh.

"Then what?" said Miles Calmer. "What can we do?"

Sir Archibald stretched out his arms with his palms flat on the table. He began to drum his fingers. "This man," he said, and his fingers were still. "Slocum, the one who rescued the Kincaid boy. It has occurred to me that we might be able to use him."

"He is no man to mess with, that one," Fahnstock said with a wry smile on his face as he looked around the table.

"What if he doesn't cooperate?" Fanting asked.

Sir Archibald's eyes lighted up. "Then—then we shall have to convince him." Then, nodding briefly to them, he pushed back his chair. "I shall keep you posted, gentlemen. Just wanted to be sure that we're all together here. And . . . uh . . ." He raised his head so that he was looking directly at them. "All of this is in absolute secrecy."

As they walked out, Sir Archibald smiled. He had certainly brought their interest and their cooperation to a peak. For he now had their tacit agreement.

When the four visitors had left, Sir Archibald walked into a room at the other end of the house where Matt

Kahane was waiting for him.

Sir Archibald Tyrell's eyes were suddenly flashing. "What's this I hear about Weber sending men to shoot up Slocum? And getting their arses burned for their trouble. That idiot!"

"I didn't know about it till after. Weber and the men were scouting the Kincaid place looking for Cullen, like you ordered. I guess they just happened to cut Slocum's trail."

"And did they find out anything about Cullen?"

"No, they didn't."

"The bloody fools!" Sir Archibald stamped his foot. "I want Slocum. I want you to bring him here."

"That will be my pleasure." Kahane's hard, pale face broke into a grin.

Matt Kahane was no coward, but he didn't like what he saw now in Sir Archibald's eyes. He had never seen an expression like that in a human face.

"Kahane, you will bring him here because *I* want to speak to him. *I* want him! Later, when everything is settled, you can do what you want with the man. But first, I want Slocum here, separated from Cullen. God damn it, man, we've got to get our hands on those land grants. God damn that fool Weber!" He paused. "I shall be busy for a couple of hours. Find me later. I want to talk to you."

And he stood there staring into the surly face of the gambler who was also his chief regulator, a title he had conferred on Kahane, until the other man dropped his eyes and turned and walked out of the room.

Sir Archibald remained where he was standing, lost in thought. All at once a smile began to spread over his face. As he walked toward the door of the room, his thoughts were not within a thousand miles of Matt Kahane, Red Weber, or the cattle war that was brewing.

The sunlight had slipped away from the windowsill and now as shadows began to claim the room the naked figures on the big bed stirred.

"Bunny, I want some more," the girl said.

Sir Archibald Tyrell ran the tip of his tongue along his lips. A smile touched the edges of his closed eyes. "My dear, you are delightfully insatiable. But I have given you all I have for the moment."

She had reached over and covered his penis with her hand. Instantly he began to stir.

"Liar," she whispered, tickling his ear, first with the breath of her single word, then with her tongue.

"Are you disappointed?"

"Let me show you how disappointed I am." She rose onto her elbow, then bent over him, taking his slowly growing member in her mouth again.

"My God, what delight!"

Her voice was muffled by the growing erection in her mouth, but he didn't care what she said as she began to suck slowly, tickling her tongue up and down his thick shaft.

"Natasha, darling." He took her head in his hands and drew her up beside him.

"Don't you want it like that, Bunny?"

"I want the two of you," he whispered. "I want both. I need it so badly that way."

"Roe has gone for a ride, Bunny. Be patient. We can wait till she gets back." But as she spoke she was stroking him with her hand, bringing his erection into ever greater readiness.

"I can't wait, Natasha, my dear. Oh, my God, what exquisite delight!"

He grabbed her buttocks suddenly and pulled her around. She came willingly to straddle him. She rode him furiously. Bunny—Sir Archibald Tyrell—came and came, with his thoughts on Roe and how he would do it with the two of them later that night.

As he rode up the long winding trail to the cabin that lay directly under the rimrocks across from the Broken Hat, Slocum thought of Boone and his brothers, of Boone saying that Millicent's place was rough to get to but great once you made it.

While they were having coffee in the pre-dawn, Slocum had pointed out that Millicent's would have been about the first place Kahane and Weber would have looked for Nat Cullen.

"Especially since I hear he was a partner," he'd said.

"They did," Boone agreed.

Kelly picked it up. "Nat figured on that. But he's got a place he hangs out there, hides."

"Plus," put in Ives, "you can see anybody coming for half a day 'fore they get there. Exceptin' at night."

"Can't anybody come in over the top of the rimrocks?" Slocum had asked.

"Could," Boone allowed, "but he'd be in a helluva shape time he got to the place." He grunted out a humorless laugh. "That there place is better forted up natural than even this here. Your friend Nat knew his ass from a hole in the ground, and that is a gut."

"I dunno about now," Ives said darkly. "Shot up; likely won't make it."

"Shut up," Boone said, but without rancor.

They had told him of the plan for an early roundup, a whole month ahead of the regular, legal gather. It was good thinking, and they could do it, being small and so more mobile than the big outfits. They would start the gather next week, Kelly had said, even sooner if they could. Meanwhile, they could expect plenty of trouble. Kahane and Weber were still looking for Cullen; in fact, that might be how they had stumbled on Slocum down below on the trail.

"Course, they could of bin intending to get you, looking for you as well as Cullen," Boone said with a chuckle. "Dumb sons of bitches didn't know what they wuz grabbin'!"

"Kahane wasn't with them, though?" Ives asked.

"Right. And I'm not too sure about Weber. I was pretty sure I heard him, but that was just when I got hit."

"They'll be back."

"Why is Kahane so hot to find Cullen?" Slocum asked.

"It's Tyrell," Ives said.

"But why?"

"You ask Cullen," Boone said. And that had been the end of that.

Then Boone had leaned forward, pouring coffee into Slocum's mug.

"I'll beat the shit out of you one day, Slocum; after we get done with the roundup; but meantime, how about coming over, come work with us. We need a man who ain't too particular how he fights," he added, sour as a lemon.

Slocum had canted his head at that. "I have turned down a job offer from Bigelow, now I got one from you. No." He shook his head.

"Just don't go workin' for that son of a bitch Tyrell,

then," Boone said, "or I won't wait till after the branding."

A laugh broke from Slocum as he watched the grim look on Boone Kincaid's face. "If they ever ask me, I'll remember to tell them you said that." He paused. "Or—I might take them up if they make me a good offer. Just to goose you boys along a little. I don't even take myself for granted, so I sure wouldn't advise you to."

Now, as he rode up the thin, hard trail toward Millicent's log house, he was thinking of the Kincaids and how simple they were. All they really seemed to want was to run some cattle, have some fun, some fighting and screwing, just like so many young bucks who punched cows and busted horses. And why not?

It was a clear day with the sun a white disc overhead in the great blue sky. A large white cloud was just over the rimrocks above Millicent's place. From Slocum's angle of vision below, it looked as if the cloud had bellied right onto the rocks. The air was dry and thin. He watched two mule deer bouncing away as he approached, their tails high in the air. A coyote sat in the shade of a rock watching him from a safe distance. He remembered old Whiskey Bill Chuckles down in Medicine Bow, who'd had a pet coyote he'd raised from a pup. His name was Pepe, and Pepe was a real sweetheart; Whiskey Bill was proud as a mother how he'd caught the pup and raised him and "civilized the son of a bitch, by God!" Until the day something happened, nobody knew what, and Pepe suddenly raised up and tore Whiskey Bill's trigger finger right out at the roots when he reached to pet him. Bill didn't waste any time in surprise. His cross-draw was fast enough to get his Colt out with his left and blast that animal to wherever untrustworthy coyotes went when they doublecrossed you. Later, over the years, Bill got maybe more fun out of telling the story of Pepe's unfaithfulness than he had had bragging about Pepe being such a civilized hound when he was alive.

The trail now led right into a stand of spruce and pine at the edge of the high timber. He walked the horse slowly, the same blue roan he'd rented from the old hostler at the livery in Cole City. Presently they broke out into the open and looked across level ground to the sturdy log cabin with the rickety porch tacked onto the front. Close by were the round horse corral and a barn. There were some other corrals on the far side of the cabin, with cattle in them, about a dozen head. In the corral by the house he saw no horses and figured maybe it was too early for business. But he knew that was nonsense, for it was never too early for fun and games, or too late either. Then, as he got closer, he saw the dappled gray horse hitched to a railing at the back of the cabin, and on the far side of him, a sorrel with a clipped left ear. Both were saddled, but he could tell they'd been there a while. Early customers? he wondered. Or did they belong to Millicent and the other girl? The Kincaids had told him that there was an extra girl working with Millicent, but that usually she worked alone.

Slocum had asked if the Box Circle riders frequented the place and Boone had told him, "Not of late." It was clear whose side Millicent was on in the cattle troubles.

Things were surely getting rough when the boys couldn't share the same cathouse, Slocum reflected as he rode up to the front of the cabin. There was nothing on the porch save a wooden chair with no back and only three legs. As he swung down from the roan he loosened the thong on his gun hammer and flexed his fingers. The stiffness was gone from them now, after the fighting at the Pick-Em-Up. Pausing for a moment close to his horse, he looked over the top of his saddle to his back trail, then let his eyes sweep along the timber line. Nothing. But he knew he must have been seen from inside the cabin. This was verified when the door opened and a woman with a hefty bust stepped out, her voice booming at him, "How do, stranger? Come on in!"

She was already on the porch as she spoke, and now two men came out the door behind her, just getting by her without brushing. Touching their hatbrims to her profile, they made for their horses at the back of the cabin. Cow waddies.

"Ma'am..." Slocum tipped his hat as he stepped up onto the porch.

"What can I do for you, mister?"

"First I could handle a whiskey and then I want to talk. You Millicent?"

"Did you think I was General Grant, for Christ's sake!" She looked at him like he was a rattler, then turned and led the way inside.

It was in that sudden turn that something caught him. An angle of her jaw, the lobe of her ear, the light— something—something there was different. He couldn't have said what. But he had the definite feeling that he had seen Millicent someplace before.

He was still puzzling this when he walked over to the bar. She poured him a drink while he had a closer look. She was a big woman, in her thirties. Parts of her were attractive when seen separately—her eyes, her haunches—but the total impression she gave was one of plainness. And yet there was clearly a warmth in her, and certainly she was lively. He had gathered from the Kincaids that Millicent was popular, and not merely because of the goods she traded in; men liked her. She was rough, and always ready with a comeback, and, as he had discovered, a racy tongue. But there was no meanness in her.

"That'll cost you money," she said as she pushed the glass toward him. "You the law?"

"No. Are you?"

"Don't try to be funny. You here to get laid? What's your name?"

"Slocum. I'm looking for Nat Cullen."

"Huh. Slocum, huh? How do I know that?"

"You don't. But Cullen knows me. Where is he?" He suddenly looked directly into her eyes. They were large, blue, and he felt there was a smile behind them. She had firm breasts, and he was glad to see she wore loose clothing. On closer view her figure was full, mobile, and capable-looking.

"So you're looking for Mr. Cullen."

"That is so."

"He ain't here. I dunno where the fuck he went, but I ain't seen him this good while."

"You know him, then?"

"He was a customer here. Can't say I knew him. You can figure he is long gone." As she spoke from behind the small bar, she ran a heavy rag across the polished wood.

Slocum tried the whiskey. "Good whiskey," he said.

"I make it myself. Three quarters river water, half a dozen rattlesnake assholes, and eagle piss." She burst into laughter at her own humor.

Slocum could do nothing but follow suit.

"I don't charge much," she said suddenly, looking at the middle of his chest.

"I'm used to getting it for free," Slocum said.

"Uh-uh. That's bad for business. A girl starts that kind of thing, it'll lead to ruin in no time." She moved down the bar.

He had a moment to look around the room. It was larger than he had thought from the outside of the cabin. The ceiling was low. There was a wheel of fortune on one wall, three tables with chairs, and some chips for poker. Two doors at one end of the cabin were closed, but he figured these for bedrooms. Or maybe one of them was a kitchen. There was another closed door at the far end of the room. There was no upstairs. A jumbo stove stood in the center of the room and a coal-oil lamp hung down from the ceiling. There were also lamps on two of the tables and one behind the bar. The place was surprisingly clean.

Suddenly he heard her swear as she dropped something. Her back was to him and as she bent down to pick up whatever it was she had dropped, he was swept again by something in her movement. "I spend all my time cleaning this fucking place," she said as she turned back to him and placed the deck of cards on the edge of the bar. In the next moment the mystery of her familiarity was settled.

Slocum heard the door open behind him and smelled the perfume that was so very faint and reminded him of someone else.

"Hello, Mr. Slocum. We meet again."

And he turned, forcing himself to keep his surprise well hidden as he faced Rhonda Haven. She was wearing skin-tight fawn-colored riding breeches and a tight lemon silk shirt. Her soft loose brown hair seemed to have been blown about her shoulders and her very white throat.

"Thought I'd run into you again, honey."

"Mister," said the voice behind him. "My sister doesn't like to be called honey. Her name is Rhonda, if you've already met, like you seem; or it's safer to call her Miss Haven."

Slocum grinned. "Can I buy you both a drink?"

Millicent moved behind the bar, her big hand reaching for the bottle and some glasses. "That you may. But we had better have one thing clear, mister." She bent slightly to assist the precision of her pouring. "My sister is a visitor to the wild West; she is not part of the establishment." She straightened and her eyes looked at him like a pair of bullets. "You got it?"

He had watched the girl color as her sister spoke.

"Millie, please . . ."

"Just want this feller to be clear."

"And I want you to be clear," Slocum said suddenly. "Just let go of your hard-on. I already told you I don't pay for it, and I don't steal it. You understand me?"

Millicent was already grinning. "By God, I am happy to see you really got balls in those big pants, Slocum. This drink now is on me."

And even though Rhonda was blushing at her sister's and Slocum's conversation, she could hardly keep the laughter out of her eyes.

7

Even before he saw him Slocum heard Cullen's rasping breath. It sounded like an old bucksaw he remembered from his childhood.

Only his gray face, framed with gray hair, real ganted now, was visible as it lay on the pillow; while the thin, reduced body lying under the bedcovers gave an impression more of absence than presence. His eyes were closed. He appeared to be sleeping. There wasn't much light in the room; the single window was facing east.

Millicent put the lamp on the table beside the bed and stood looking down at her patient. Rhonda had remained in the front room.

"He doesn't look too good," Slocum said.

"What did you expect?" she said, her tone surly.

"Doc seen him?"

"He comes by. He says he's..." She didn't finish, but out of the side of his eye Slocum saw the slight shrug of her shoulders.

"How come the Box Circle men didn't find him here?

I heard Kahane and Weber were hot after him."

"We've got a hiding place. Luckily I saw them coming, and we had time."

"Can he walk? Move around?"

Slocum had pulled up the one chair in the room. Now he sat down.

"If you help him, now and again. Like to the outhouse, or he takes a leak out the back door. Or I got that pot there."

"Doc get all the lead out?"

"Enough to start a mine," she said. "But, by God, he went down fighting."

A gurgling sound came from the bed. And now Slocum realized the figure had begun to speak, but it was difficult to know what it was saying.

"Take it slow, Nat baby. Your friend Slocum's here." Millicent had leaned forward and put her hand on Cullen's forehead. "Hot as a pistol, for Christ's sake," she muttered in disgust.

"So's my whanger," said the voice weakly. And his eyes opened to stare like dull marbles at his visitors as Millicent turned up the lamp.

"Hello, Nat. It's John Slocum."

"I know yer name." And the wan face tried to fall into a grin, but was having difficulty.

"When does the doc come again?" Slocum asked.

"Likely any day. He ain't reg'lar. And, course, he has got to be careful nobody sees him comin' out here." Millicent reached over and scratched her left shoulder.

Slocum said, "Maybe he could use a drink?"

"Maybe we all could," Millicent said, turning quickly and leaving the room.

The man in the bed continued to stare at Slocum.

"Well, John, it has been a while."

"Sure has."

"Not a helluva lot different than the goddamn army."

"I hear you burned down a few of them."

"You bet yer ass."

"I met Kahane and Weber."

This time the grin was a little firmer, and the two of them waited as the door opened in silence, feeling the strange moment until Millicent came in with whiskey and glasses. Briskly she poured.

"By God, that's good." The man in bed gargled the words as the strong fluid raced through his body.

"It'll put bullets in your gun," Slocum said.

"Got that already." He tilted the glass again. Holding it on his chest now, he leered at Millicent. "We could check that out, girlie."

"You take it slow."

By now Cullen was more of his old self. "Where is that cute little sis of yours?" he asked. Looking at Slocum, he lowered one eyelid.

"You cut that shit," snapped Millicent. "Rhonda is not your sort. You leave her alone."

"Can't I even feel her with my eyes?"

"And your horny mind."

"Ain't any hornier'n yours!"

Millicent chuckled. "I see you're feeling better."

"Always do when you're about, my dear."

"Bullshit."

"Come closer. Come closer." And when she did come up close to the bed he said, "Here, put your hand down here and see what's bullshit or not."

"Honey, I see what you mean, but we'll wait till later."

"You got customers out there?" He turned his head

slightly toward Slocum. The grin was broader now. It was really there. "You thinking of Slocum here?"

"He turned me down."

Cullen started to laugh, but then coughed. His face twisted in a grimace.

"Slow down," Millicent cautioned as she took the glass of whiskey out of his hand. "Shouldn't of given you the booze, maybe."

He was wheezing, fighting for breath, but Slocum saw that he was coming out of it. There was strong color in his face.

"The whiskey sure helps, don't it," he said with a grin.

"And sex, my friend."

"I sure go with that. But don't kill yourself with your lady friend." And he winked at Millicent.

"You know a better way to die?"

It was truly amazing, Slocum was thinking, how the wan, brittle man he had seen lying in the bed gasping for breath when he'd first walked into the room had suddenly changed into almost his old self. To be sure, it brought him pain to move, but it didn't stop the sparkle which had come into his eyes.

"Doc says I'm about done for. He is full of shit."

"It is you who better not be so full of shit," snapped Millicent, coming back into the room again. "Now, where you think you're going!" Her voice rose as Cullen started to push back the bedcovers and rise up.

"I got to get up."

"Lie there. What do you want, damn it!" She turned to Slocum. "Doesn't do a damn bit of good to tell him over and over that if he wants something to tell me. Damn it, you get yer ass back in that bed!" And she almost shoved Slocum aside in her zeal to keep Cullen in bed. "See," she explained to him over her shoulder, "it's like that—one minute you figure he's cashed in, next he's trying to climb into my pants."

"Get away!" Cullen's voice was grainy but hard, and Slocum could tell he wasn't fooling. So could Millicent, and she stepped back. "You don't have to be so goddamn bossy!" He almost snarled at her. "Exceptin' when I need your helpin'," he added. "I got to do something not you nor anybody can do for me. Now git. If I need help, Slocum here'll do it. Go on! Git!"

It took him a while to get up out of the bed, and he wouldn't let her help him. He stood holding his hand against the log wall to steady himself, his breath sawing.

"I can make it," he said, seeing the look on Slocum's face. "Got to get practice on it. Those buggers'll be back. I got to be ready." He paused, sucking breath. Then, "You come, though, in case I need a hand."

It took a while to make it to the outhouse and back, but Cullen did it under his own power. When he was in bed again, he closed his eyes.

"Shut the door," he said softly. "Don't want anybody in—to come..."

For a while he slept. His head lolled. He began to snore. Slocum got up and walked out of the room.

The front room was deserted, and when he saw the horse outside, he realized Millicent had a customer. He wondered where Rhonda was. While he'd been with Cullen he hadn't had room in his thoughts for her, but now she came strongly into his mind as he stepped outside the cabin. Unhitching the roan, he led him into the round horse corral. He stripped him and began rubbing him down with some twigs he'd found, and then with a cloth which he took from his possibles bag, tied to the saddle skirt.

He had just finished when he heard a horse approaching. It was Rhonda, smiling at him as she slipped down from the saddle.

"Can we talk, Slocum?" she asked.

"I've been waiting this good while," he said amiably. He started to the barn, leading the blue roan and packing his saddle and bridle over his shoulder. In the barn he found oats and hay, then showed the girl how to rub down her horse and feed him. They didn't speak, attending to the work at hand.

The sun stood behind the horizon when they came outside again. His eyes scanned the darkened timber line.

"How do you find your friend?" she asked.

"Different." He gave a wry little laugh. "But I guess I'm different to him, too."

"I was angry with you on the stagecoach."

"I sure wouldn't have guessed it."

She laughed at that. It was the first time he had heard her laugh. It seemed to ring all the way through her. It wasn't a belly laugh like Millicent's; it sounded like a song.

"How long are you going to stay out here?" he asked.

"Not long. I came out to tell Millie about our mother and father." She paused. "Mother died just over a year ago, and Father only a month later. I had trouble finding Millie. She hadn't written in ever so long. I'd no idea where she was. Anyhow, not to go into a long story, I located her and came out."

"Was she expecting you?"

"No." They had been walking slowly away from the barn and cabin, and now she stopped. They were halfway to the timber line. "No." Her eyes looked up into his, and he saw the tears that stood there but didn't fall. "I don't know that she would have had me out if she'd known I wanted to come."

"Was she glad to see you?"

"I don't know." She turned her head. "She's . . . well . . . older, as you can tell. We were never very close, but I always admired Millie. She left home, though, long ago. When I was little." She was looking down at her hands, which she was holding together at her waist. "I always wanted really to know my sister. But now I don't know if I did the right thing. I rather think not. We were a . . . a proper family, I guess you'd call us. We went to church, and all that. Our parents were very religious. A little too much so. I suspect that was why Millie left. She just left. She ran away. And—and I—I'm beginning to think now maybe she didn't want me to find her. But . . ." Her voice trailed off and, seeing her bent head turned away from him, he knew she was weeping.

"But you wanted to tell her about your mother and father," Slocum said. She was crying too hard to answer, and could only nod, holding her thumb knuckle in her mouth like a little girl. In a moment she stopped and straightened her shoulders.

"But don't misunderstand. Millie has been wonderful in the short time I've been here. Wonderful." She was wiping tears from her face with the back of her hand and wrist. "And—and I'm glad I found her. I like her. I like her a lot."

"I've a notion she likes you," Slocum said. "Don't mind the way she talks."

Suddenly she gave a giggle. "I think some of it's kind of funny, actually." Then she said, "The rest . . . I don't know." And her face was sad again. "The rest is not so funny."

They had resumed walking and were now at the line of trees. He stopped and touched her arm. "Try to understand her," he said. "There's nothing to criticize. Millie is a good woman. You can tell that, can't you?"

She was nodding, too choked again with tears to reply in words.

Slocum looked back at the cabin, wondering if anyone was watching. The saddle horse was still outside, hitched to the rail. Maybe the visitor was having a drink, or maybe going for seconds. He could feel his passion mounting for the girl beside him, and he had to restrain himself from slipping his arm around her. But Millicent just could be watching, and this was no time to run afoul of her. He might be needing her as Nat Cullen did.

"Come on," he said. "I'll walk you back. I need to talk to Cullen about some things."

They took only a few minutes to reach the cabin, with the early night closing out the rimrocks on the other side of the valley. He wondered how the Kincaids were doing. Right damn soon they'd be making their gather and then hell would pop.

The little sorrel mare hitched outside the cabin was swaybacked and Slocum noted she was blind in one eye. Surely no cowhand was riding such an old crowbait. The minute he walked in the door and heard the wet, coughing laughter he knew who it was.

"Well, bless my soul! John Slocum himself in person. I declare, it is my day of privilege, sir!" Colonel Quimby Hounds rose like a new dawn out of the chair from which he had been regaling Millicent with colorful, racy, and of course a goodly number of apocryphal stories. His

114

hand swept upward in an authentic Confederate salute. "Sir! I insist on this round!" His head whipped to the bar. "My good Millicent, will you bring liquid refreshment for my friend, and this gorgeous young lady. I am Colonel Quimby Hounds, Miss . . . uh . . ."

"Rhonda Haven, Colonel Hounds."

And Slocum smiled at the way she picked up on the colonel's game. Seeing the scowl on Millicent's face, he laughed. "Come on, Millicent. I trust the colonel was a gentleman."

"Damn it to hell! That's the trouble with the old codger!" she snapped out. Hounds and Slocum both roared, while Millicent joined them, seating herself at the table. Rhonda seemed to Slocum to be looking nowhere.

"I had no idea I would run into you here, Slocum." The colonel was beaming all around himself. "Or rather, in a way, I did. Yes, I did. And have you found what you were after?"

"Yes, I have, Colonel," Slocum replied, with his eyes on the girl's soft profile.

"And what were you looking for, you dirty man?" demanded Millicent. "Be careful!" she warned, and her scowl was thunderous.

Slocum regarded her with eyes as innocent as a newborn. "Why, for heaven. I was looking for heaven. And I found it."

At that point the bedroom door opened and Nat Cullen stood framed in surprise, a Smith & Adams revolver in his hand.

"By God, Quimby himself!"

"You get back into bed!" roared Millicent, charging to her feet.

"Only if you join me, honey."

"We'll see about that later. Now get back in there!"

"Thought maybe we had some unnecessary visitors," Cullen said, looking down at the revolver in his hand. "Man never knows." He wagged his head slowly. "Maybe I was dreaming."

"Horses!" Slocum said suddenly, pushing back his chair. "Get in your room, Cullen."

"Shit, no time to hide him," Millicent said.

"It's several," Slocum said. "Could be trouble—by the way they're riding." He looked at the girl. "You better get out of sight too," he said.

"Get in the bedroom," Millicent told her. "With those two. Slocum, get Cullen into bed. I'll handle our guests." And she was striding to the door, a big Navy Colt .45 in her fist.

Slocum had stepped quickly into the kitchen, opened the window, and slipped out to find himself standing in the full light of the moon at the rear of the cabin just as the horsemen pounded up at the front. They had come in fast and he could smell the dust the horses had churned up, and now their sweat.

He had acted quickly, knowing that if he waited he could easily be boxed into the cabin, a target. And at the moment there was nothing to be done about getting Cullen out.

Hugging the cabin, he eased his way toward one of the front corners. Using a rain barrel as cover, he made out the four riders at the front of the house. Someone was cursing and the horses were breathing heavily. There was much jangling of metal bits and the creak of leather. For the moment no sound was coming from inside the cabin. He could imagine the girl and Quimby Hounds in the room with Cullen, and Millicent at the door, with her handgun, ready for the visitors. But nobody started shooting and in a moment he saw a big man who could have been Red Weber dismount and walk onto the porch. Another man followed while the remaining two stayed in their saddles.

The shorter man unfolded a paper he had taken from his pocket and while he held it against the logs alongside the door, his companion began nailing it to the cabin wall, using the butt of his sixgun as a hammer.

Suddenly Millicent's abrasive voice came cracking through the closed door. "What the hell you buggers doin' out there? What's that hammering? You fuckers git on your hosses or I am going to start throwing lead!"

The hammering continued, and suddenly bullets began to blast through the door of the cabin, while Millicent's roar almost drowned out the sound of the gunfire. The horses meanwhile had spooked and the men had trouble handling them.

"I told you sons of bitches to haul ass! I know there is four of you out there, and you can sure outgun me. Question is, which two, maybe three of you shitheads I'm gonna take with me when I open this door!"

"Red, for Christ's sake, let's get outta here," one of the horsemen blurted, turning his horse out of the range of gunfire.

"Hold it!" Weber snapped as he made one final strike with his gun butt. Then he turned and ran to his horse. His companion was already in the saddle. And now, mounted, Weber turned and fired at the cabin door. None of his companions followed suit.

"Fuck you, you goddamn whore!" he shouted. He

kicked his horse into a gallop and the four night riders drummed across the open land and disappeared down the trail. Shots continued to come from the staunch, irate, and irrevocable Millicent inside the cabin.

When the firing stopped, Slocum walked up and pulled the notice from the wall and called out to Millicent not to shoot. In a moment he stood facing the furious lady of the house.

"So why didn't you ventilate the sons of bitches, Slocum?"

"They weren't doing any harm, so why invite the whole of the Box Circle outfit over for a range war, you dumb shit." He glared at her, though not without humor in his eyes.

"What's that thing in your hand?"

He held it up and began to read as the colonel and Rhonda came into the front room, followed more slowly by Cullen.

"It says: 'Rustlers, horse thieves, and such killers will be shot on sight, or hanged. You bastards start praying. Cole County Vigilance Committee.'"

A moment of silence followed the reading. Then, abruptly, Millicent stepped to the bar and they heard the familiar sounds of bottle and glasses.

"Looks like they're putting that notice around the countryside," the colonel said.

Millicent was looking at her sister. "Honey, I want you to get the first stage out of here. Now, I know..." She held up both palms of her big hands to ward off the objection she felt was forthcoming. "I know you want to be with your big sister, but we can wait to be together when this shenanigans blows over. Lying side by side in

118

a pair of pine boxes isn't the way I see being together. Now I mean that!"

Slocum watched the girl bite her lower lip.

"Listen to Millicent," the colonel said.

"That's the first sensible thing I've heard you say," Millicent boomed out, and poured extra whiskey into Quimby Hounds's glass.

"My pleasure, ma'am," the colonel said, his little finger at a rakish angle as he lifted the glass of brown liquid.

"I will leave if you come with me," Rhonda said, and Slocum felt the jolt in him. There was a lot more than just a little of her older sister in her, he realized.

"You ought to do what they say," he said, looking right into the girl's face. "Those men are killers. You saw some of them when you were on the stage."

"I believe the lass should make up her own mind," Cullen said suddenly. He reached out and tried to slip his arm around her waist.

"Get your pickin' paws off of that," snarled Millicent, "or I will put a few dozen more holes in you!"

This observation brought a tremendous sigh of resignation from Cullen, and drove Quimby Hounds into a severe attack of coughing laughter.

"The course of true love is never easy," Slocum said. "Cullen, my friend, the lady is crazy for you, so you had better do what she says."

"You tellin' me something, Slocum?"

Slocum felt the steel in Cullen's words and he watched him carefully now as he spoke. "I sure am. I am telling you not to be a damn fool."

The two men who had fought together not so very

long ago, who had gone through so much, stared at each other. A long moment passed while the colonel had another drink of his whiskey, and the women kept their eyes away from the tableau that had suddenly and so dramatically appeared. Hounds of course was watching too, for here, as he would have put it himself, here was "major news;" but not wishing to get involved, he kept his eyes loose, not staring at the two men, but taking it all in nonetheless.

Finally Cullen dropped his eyes. "Good enough, Slocum," he said. "Good enough." And without another word he turned and walked slowly into his room.

"You are a tough son of a bitch, ain't'cha, Mr. Slocum?" Millicent leaned over and spat into a cuspidor that was nearby.

"You are half right, lady. You can say I am tough. I wouldn't say the rest again. If you want to talk and act like a man, then you better be ready to pay for it." He smiled at her, a fresh, open smile that lit up his whole face. "Can't help liking you, Millicent." To Rhonda he said, "But I do believe your sister might get the wrong idea if I let you . . . or anybody . . . talk to me like that."

"You know I let you take that one for old times' sake; and on account of keeping friendly relations in this rough time." Nat Cullen was lying propped up on his bed as he regarded his old war companion.

"About time we had a talk, wouldn't you say?"

"I appreciate your coming."

"Didn't have anything better to do," Slocum told him.

Cullen grinned, then winced. "Still not all glued together," he said, "but it is coming."

"Is this the place you were doing your business with?" Slocum asked.

"I throwed in with Millicent. Then when I got shot up I had to let her take over. But you see how some women are. You give 'em an inch and they want it all."

Slocum grinned. "A woman like that I can believe you'd be wanting to give it all."

Cullen would have laughed at that, but he was hurting.

"You're going to make it," Slocum said. "We had worse, didn't we?"

"We sure did."

"So what do you want me for?"

"I need a pardner."

"You've got Millicent."

"I don't mean for this here." His eyes swept the room. "There is talk, more than talk, of the railroad running a spur out here. It would change the town, make it a shipping point, and would also make a lot of rich men. You get the drift."

"I do. But I'm what they call the footloose type, Cullen. I don't stay long in any one place. You know that. You are that way yourself."

"I don't mean stay forever, but while there's the action. We could have a real good time."

"Who knows about the railroad?"

"Nobody. Except probably there are some who do," he added.

"How do you know?"

"While I was doing my duty as sheriff of Cole County one day I happened to be riding out toward the Twin Buttes and right there alongside the trail was a mail sack. Been dropped after a holdup."

121

"Huh." Slocum reached for a quirly while the man on the bed paused for breath.

"In it was a letter to a feller named Bill Tolson. The letter was from a man high up in the U.P. Tolson was head of the bank in Cole City. But the letter never got to him and Tolson is dead."

"Shot?"

"Accident."

"What did the letter say?"

"That the spur was planned, and there was a whole thing about buying up property. Now, I got the paper that shows just what property is the best to buy according to where the railroad will run."

"It was in the letter?"

"No, no. The U.P. man was smarter than that. It was referred to in the letter, but only as a reference to information coming under separate cover." He paused. "I took a chance, and found the stage driver who'd been held up. There had been money aboard, but he'd had this special letter he was carrying. They didn't get that." He paused. "It was a hunch, but it paid off."

"Did he know what was in it?"

"He'd opened it, but without the other letter it was just a list of names and some drawings. Didn't mean much of anything without the first letter."

"So he gave it to you."

"I was the law. I needed all the evidence. And, as you know, besides that, I can be persuasive."

Slocum grinned.

"Somehow Tyrell or Kahane—it doesn't matter— found out I had this. I figure something leaked from the stage driver. It doesn't matter. It's why they're so hot after me; though that son of a bitch Weber has his private reasons." He paused. "The more I think about it, the more I wonder if Bill Tolson wasn't killed."

"So you want me to help you put the deal through, and then ride off."

"You could deal your own hand. I need you. I can't pull this off alone. Especially like this."

Slocum said nothing. Then, "But without realizing what was going on right under your feet you got yourself stuck in a range war."

A wry grin broke out all over Cullen's face, and he even looked sheepish. "Reminds me of the time I was having some fun with a lady when her husband came home unexpected and in the dark I ran right smack into a clothesline."

Both of them broke into laughter, Cullen doubling with pain, but still figuring it was worth it.

"I got to sleep now," Cullen said, and his voice was weak.

"I'll be riding over to the Box Circle in the morning," Slocum said. "Might see something on Tyrell. And I've got a date with Kahane anyway."

But Nat Cullen was already asleep, a snore rolling out of his loose, dry lips.

8

He lay in his bedroll on the fresh ground at the edge of
the timber line some distance from the cabin, smelling the pine and fir and spruce, and the sage too. Whenever the wind stirred gently he could smell the blue roan,
which he had picketed close by. He lay there in the
echoing silence of the great mountains that ringed him
and his world, listening, feeling the life of the great land
and sky.

He had chosen to sleep outside the cabin in case more
visitors decided to pay a call. At the same time, he
preferred sleeping outdoors, preferred the ground to a
bed. It seemed to him this night was especially still, and
he could hear her coming out of the cabin. He waited,
hoping it was Rhonda, yet knowing it would not be.

"I almost fell asleep waiting for you," he said as she
stood by the bedroll, looking down at him.

"Hoping it was Rhonda, I'll bet'cha!"

"Sure was. But it isn't, so you'll have to do." He had
not moved, but remained lying on his back, with his

hands together behind his head.

"Bastard." But he could hear no anger in her voice. Then she said, "I didn't come out here for that. I . . ."

She stopped and he asked, "What did you come for, then?"

"I dunno." She squatted down, her elbows on her knees. "Maybe I was lonely. How the hell do I know!"

For a moment he thought she was going to leave; he could feel her struggling with something. After a long moment of silence she spoke.

"You know Cullen's my man. We have been partners in bed too. He is one helluva man!"

"I won't argue that. What's your drift?"

"Cullen is kind of stove up now. Temporary. But still stove." And then she added, "Least I hope it is temporary."

"He'll make it."

"Will you help him, Slocum? He can't go it alone. Tyrell and Kahane will catch up with him sooner or later for sure."

She was looking down at him as they spoke and now, like a bell, he felt something ring all the way through him. He sat up and pushed his hat out of the way and moved a little so there was room beside him.

"What're you doing?"

"Why don't you just shut up and take your clothes off?"

In the next minute they were lying naked beside each other.

"Slocum . . ."

He turned his head toward her and in the clear, high air he could see her well enough even though there was no moon. Suddenly he realized that she was crying.

"What's the matter?"

"Nothing. God damn it. Nothing!" Then, "I was thinking of my sister, my kid sister. I'm glad she's not like me."

Slocum had the strange feeling that a much younger woman than Millicent had spoken. He leaned over now and touched the tears away from her cheeks with his fingers. Her hand came up and held his; somehow, her hand seemed not so big now as when he had looked at her earlier in the cabin.

"She is like you, Millie."

"How do you mean that?"

"She's a decent girl."

"Shit, Slocum, you know I'm just a goddamn whore! What the hell you talking about!"

"I said she's a decent girl, and that she's like you, a decent woman. Now shut up. Words get between people. Don't you know that by now?"

They lay there naked beside each other for a very long moment while he could feel his body opening, and hers too, and his erection thrust against her soft thigh.

Presently she reached down and slid her hand around his great, hard organ, and he started to rise up onto his knees.

Her voice was almost a whisper, and fell against him like air. "I don't want you inside me; that's for Cullen. Can I have you like this?"

Slocum understood, and she knew he did, for she didn't wait for an answer.

The light was just starting to change the sky as he awakened. He had not slept deeply, but rather had spent the night at that level of resting that he practiced on the trail, neither wholly asleep nor completely awake, but with his senses alert to sounds, changes in the atmosphere, smells, and shifts in the wind.

He had put on his clothes as soon as Millicent had left the night before, and had slept in them, with his Colt close to his hand. Now he awakened as easily as he had slept. Quickly he rolled his bedding, tied it onto the saddle skirt, and checked the roan's rigging. He didn't build a fire, but ate as he rode: beef jerky and some jawbreaker candy he'd bought back in Junction Crossing. He was soon out of sight of the cabin. It didn't look like anyone was up yet.

As he rode into the slipping dawn he wondered again what he was doing here, spending the night out at Millicent's and Cullen's whorehouse in the Rockies, getting mixed up in a cattle fight. Slocum was not one to keep accounts with friends or even acquaintances, and yet Nat Cullen had helped him out of that tight those years ago. And so he had come to Cole City, to the Flint River. Good enough. But how much was good enough? He was beginning to ask himself now.

Plainly Archibald Tyrell was throwing a real wide loop, playing for much bigger stakes than the stockmen. He would use their force against the mavericers to pull off his deal with the railroad, clear the land of the rustler trouble and build the town. It would be an easy breeze for the Chelting Company then, by God, once Tyrell had his hands on those land grants.

Yet Slocum had no interest in partnering Cullen. He'd pay his debt and then he'd move on. The cattle fight wasn't his fight. It didn't concern him who won out, and it sure didn't concern him if Cole City became a real town or just blew off the prairie. Yes, the Kincaids wanted him, and so did J. J. Bigelow. Maybe even Tyrell would want him, for all he knew. Slocum didn't care. He didn't give a damn who wanted him or needed him; all that concerned him was having himself, his own self, any time he needed. Like now.

He would side Cullen for long enough to be quits. And maybe he'd find time for some sport with the girls— Millicent, the blonde in the San Francisco House, and especially Rhonda. Especially the brown-haired, brown-eyed Rhonda Haven, who he definitely felt had started to open to him. Of course, you never knew, there might be someone else showing up.

It was just then, at a turn in the trail, that the three riders rode at him with guns drawn. Slocum saw it was useless to resist. They had been waiting between a cut-bank and some box elders, but because of the slight haze coming off the wet early morning grass and the angle at which the trail approached this particular spot, the relationship between the cutbank and the trees had fooled him. It was narrower than it appeared.

"Sir Archibald Tyrell wants to see you," said the familiar voice.

"I'll give him a few minutes of my time," Slocum said, speaking with soft ease, as the riders moved in closer and Red Weber brought his red-streaked eyes to bear directly on the man who had twice humiliated him— at the Pick-Em-Up and at the trail leading to the Kincaids'.

"You must realize," Sir Archibald Tyrell was saying, "that the country will be on our side. They want to get rid of the rustlers as badly as we do."

Matt Kahane, seated in the big leather chair opposite

his employer, nodded slowly. "Right. Right, and they'll appreciate our doing most of the dirty work, hiring guns and all that."

"The small man, the average man, wants peace, Kahane. And he doesn't care how he gets it."

"Things are well under control." Kahane could never bring himself to call Tyrell "Sir Archibald," especially to his face, so he left the place for such words carefully blank.

Sir Archibald, of course, was well aware of the problem, and he relished it, as he always found pleasure in other people's discomfort.

Kahane had lighted one of his own cigars, as Sir Archibald had not offered him one from the silver box on his desk. Smoking slowly, he watched his employer the way a careful man will watch someone dealing cards. After all, Kahane was a gambler.

"We have sent men to invite Slocum for a talk," he said. "They should be about making contact now."

Sir Archibald nodded. "Good."

"I don't know why you think you need him," Kahane said, and he emphasized his displeasure by brushing the fallen cigar ash off his clothes, letting it fall about the room.

Sir Archibald scowled, but otherwise refused to show the displeasure that went much deeper than that. He was tired of Kahane, and of Red Weber too. The men were pushy, and Kahane was dark and mysterious as well. Well, he would use them. It was his rule: how to make use of someone, of a situation. For everyone and everything could be used sooner or later.

"Why do I want to talk with him?" Sir Archibald drummed his fingers along the top of his mahogany desk and surveyed big Matt Kahane. "He is better on our side than on theirs, for one thing," he said. "So they will have him the less, so to put it. And then, he might wish to work for us. I hear he is pretty good with his fists and with a gun." He smiled maliciously at the man in the leather chair.

"It would be sensible to kill him. He can cause us big trouble."

"How?"

"He already has. That's how."

"No, Kahane. He has caused *us* no trouble at all. He has caused *you* trouble and he has caused *Weber* trouble, but he has not caused me an ounce of trouble. Nor will he." And he stood up just as there came a knock at the door.

"Come."

It was a skinny man with a limp. "Red and the boys have picked up Slocum," he said, looking more at Kahane than at Tyrell. "Hinds got their signal from the Butte. They'll be riding in pretty directly."

"How soon?" snapped Sir Archibald. "Look at me when you report, mister!"

The man with the limp flushed, but more with anger than embarrassment. "I am saying, they will be here when they get here."

"File, you give Sir Archibald a time, damn it!" snapped Kahane. "Who the hell d'you think you are?"

The man named File did get red now, and it wasn't only from anger. While he had reddened more deeply, Kahane, his immediate boss, had on the other hand whitened, so that his black eyes looked like stones as he glared at File.

"I'd say half an hour."

"Get out then and let us know when they get here."

When he was gone Kahane regarded his employer with amusement. "The men are not friendly toward the English, as you can see."

"I didn't happen to notice much love lost over you, however," Sir Archibald observed icily. "That will be all, Kahane. Let me know when Slocum arrives."

The big man rose from the armchair and started to the door of the room.

"Oh, and Kahane..."

Kahane stopped with his hand on the doorknob, then turned, letting his hand fall. "What?" he said.

Sir Archibald had opened a drawer in his desk as he stood up. "Follow me a moment. I want to show you something." He brought his hand out of the drawer. He was holding a Smith & Wesson revolver.

Kahane, puzzled, but not showing it through his impassive eyes and his mask-like face, followed Sir Archibald out of the room and around to the back of the house where a shooting range was set up with targets, bottles, and other objects. There was a small shed to one side.

File had seen them leave the office and he was already there. His manner was still not servile, but he knew which side his bread was buttered. He stood by the targets, which were lined up some distance from where Sir Archibald and Kahane had stopped.

"Over there," Sir Archibald said, and he nodded to the little shed, which was built of lumber and fortified with tin.

"You've been practicing with your pistol," Kahane said with a hard laugh.

"Right you are, Kahane. I want to show you something, and you can tell some of your colleagues about it." He paused. "I know they respect me out of fear. I pay them. That's enough to get anyone to respect you up to a point. After that point, this!" And he hefted the Smith & Wesson.

"Open one hatch," he called out to File.

A moment passed, while they waited.

"Be patient," Sir Archibald said to Kahane with a laugh. "They're drowsy in there." And as he spoke something came shuttling through the hole. It was a pack rat, long, heavy, and fast. He was followed by a second rat, and a third, and a fourth.

"All right, Kahane!"

Kahane had already drawn and now he fired. The first rat exploded in blood and entrails.

Even before the echo of the gunshot had faded, Sir Archibald had fired three shots, killing the next three rats.

"Shut the door now, File!"

He turned to the man beside him, who could barely conceal his astonishment at the English dude's speed and accuracy.

"You see, Kahane, I never told you—I didn't feel it was necessary—but I am considered, and indeed I am, a crack pistol shot back home. I have more medals and other declarations to my prowess than you can count."

"Good enough shooting," Kahane said, and there was the trace of a smile on his face, though condescending and reluctant.

The gleam that came into Sir Archibald's eyes now was vicious. "But I want to show you just one thing more, Kahane, which you can pass on to Weber and the others, the gunmen you have hired for me." He called

over his shoulder, still keeping his eyes on Matt Kahane.
"Open the other door!"

This time they didn't have to wait long. Three huge
rats appeared and started to run. This time Sir Archibald
held the Smith & Wesson in his left hand. Sir Archibald
Tyrell was soft, fat, short of breath, and like no one any
of the men at the Box Circle had ever seen before, even
among the British cattlemen who were becoming more
and more numerous. He raised his handgun and fired
only three shots, hitting each of those three speeding
pack rats into total disintegration.

When he lowered the gun File, his milky eyes pop-
ping, didn't have to be told to shut the hatch.

Sir Archibald waited a moment, rather a long moment,
as he savored the intake of breath he heard from the man
standing beside him. He turned now to look with amusement into those black eyes. "You see, Kahane, *I* can do
it with either or both hands." And his eyes dropped to
the other man's empty sleeve.

As he rode down the trail with the three Box Circle riders,
Slocum's anger grew. What was especially annoying was
the fact that he had himself intended riding out to Tyrell's
outfit, and he'd been forestalled. He had decided to stay
with Cullen until he was on his feet; to help him if he
could. Indeed, he'd given Millicent his tacit agreement
on that score. That was the least he could do; once Cullen
could handle a horse and a gun he could leave. His
account would be squared. But until then his old war
companion was clearly a sitting target. The Kincaids
wouldn't be much help. Tough though the boys might
be, they'd been working with a whole lot of luck. Nor
were their fellow ranchers numerous. As far as Slocum

could figure, the small stockmen didn't have a chance. Tyrell had plenty of gunmen, and he could always hire more. The Englishman's only problem was in squaring his actions with Bigelow; that is, with the law.

As for Bigelow, the lawman could try for a straight line of law-abiding action from both parties. Not that that meant a damn once the lead started flying. But maybe he could keep the lid on. Maybe. The whole thing was a mess, no question about that.

The one clear point that was emerging was that Slocum would see Cullen through. He'd given his word, even though not spoken. He had seen acceptance in the other man's eyes. Nothing had to be said. And so, for him, the cattle fight could settle itself, the Kincaids could settle their own business with the law and with the Box Circle, and Millicent and her sister could work out whatever they had to work out. So could Cullen. So could Cullen, once he'd gotten through this tight; once he was on his feet and able to handle a gun. Slocum had no doubt Cullen could deal with Kahane and Red Weber. And if he couldn't, then—as the man said—he couldn't.

So why had he been riding to see Sir Archibald Tyrell? To lower some of the odds against Cullen? He was thinking of the silver flask; it could have been Kahane who had bushwhacked Cullen, Kahane or someone he'd hired. The stupid bastard, flashing that flask around like that. As he thought of Kahane now, Slocum realized that the gambler was really his problem, as much as, if not more than, Cullen's.

Only now Tyrell wanted him. For what? Obviously, he didn't want him dead. Not yet. For though the riders were as friendly as the guns they carried, they still hadn't roughed him up, hadn't said anything to rouse him to retaliation and so have an excuse to shoot him. What then? Clearly, Tyrell wanted to talk, and the men were simply making sure he got to the Box Circle before he might stir up any action amongst the Kincaids and mavericks. They hadn't even taken his gun, figuring a close eye on him was enough security.

And so, while they held the deck, he wasn't without anything to play. His hand wasn't empty. He didn't have any aces, but maybe he had a couple of wild deuces, he reflected as he shifted his weight in his saddle and began thinking of Denny Kincaid and his problem with horses. Remembering his own animal's bad temper, and the buffalo-skinning knife in his bedroll. And again he shifted in his saddle, grimacing as he did so, as though in pain.

"Like to step down a minute," he said, shifting again.

"You could put a cork in it," one rider said, and one of his companions gave an abrupt laugh.

"Got the piles, and they're hurtin' to beat hell. Bleeding. I'd appreciate a minute to settle some of my bedding on my saddle."

The rider he had picked to speak to sniffed, looking over at his companions. He was young, and Slocum had picked him as the accessible one.

"He's got the piles; wants to stop," the rider said, and drew rein.

"That's a pain in the ass," another man said, and the three of them laughed at that.

The others had reined in their horses now, and Slocum said mildly, "I do appreciate it." He was careful to make his descent from his saddle appear as painful as he could.

"Hurry it up," one man said. "We ain't got all day."

"Be just a minute." And he unbuckled his gunbelt and handed it to one of the riders, who was greatly surprised as he hung it over his saddlehorn. It was the move he hoped would disarm them.

They kept him in view, but he had his bandanna out, and made a good show of slipping it into his trousers as a pad. "Not very thick," he said. "I'll tie my roll on my saddle. That should do her, I reckon."

They were watching him, but not too carefully, as he went through the action of carefully placing the heavy blanket on the seat of his saddle while he slipped the knife inside the sleeve of his shirt, still distracting them with his grimaces of pain and physical difficulty.

As he gathered the reins and prepared to step into the stirrup, one of the men snarled, "Come on, we got to get going. It is getting late."

"Right with you," Slocum said, his face twisting in severe discomfort as he lifted his foot to the stirrup and Blue turned his head back to snap at him. In that precise moment he jabbed the point of the knife into the horse's ribs and swung up at the same time. Blue spun and Slocum let out a wild Texas yell as though he was going to go flying. He jabbed the animal again and Blue began kicking and bucking; he'd got his head down because Slocum had let him. The roan was spinning as Slocum jabbed again, kicking and yanking him into the knot of riders, crashing against the man who had his gunbelt hanging over his saddlehorn. Miraculously he managed to grab the gunbelt as the riders scattered.

Suddenly he let go and dropped out of his saddle, rolling into the brush at the edge of some trees. He pulled up behind a high stump, already firing the Colt, hitting one man in his gun arm. Blue meanwhile had kicked another rider in the leg.

The last rider didn't hesitate; he was already bolting

down the trail, and Slocum didn't waste a bullet on him.

Quickly he stashed his bedding, sheathed the knife, and now with a calmer Blue he stepped briskly into the saddle. Only now he was listening to the inner voice he knew so well. It was something that had always been with him: an intuition, a thing to be trusted. And he trusted it now as he turned the blue roan in the direction of the Broken Hat. It was clear that Tyrell wanted to bring him to the Box Circle for one reason only—to separate him from Cullen and the Kincaids. That could only mean that Kahane's gunmen were ready to go.

Marshal J. J. Bigelow sat in his office paring his big black fingernails. The marshal was thinking. Or—as he would have put it, and only if necessary—he was "turning it over." It was absolutely clear what his next move had to be, but he was reluctant. Not because he was afraid to die—he'd already learned to deal with that likelihood—but because he just didn't want to get over-involved in the damn cattle trouble. *The damn fools,* he was thinking, *starting their gather a month early.* Smart; but stupid too, on account of it was going to push Archibald Tyrell's hand.

The question was, should he call for the army? The obvious first move on his own part, however, was to ride out and collect young Denny Kincaid who by God was supposed to be standing trial, the circuit judge being due any day now.

J.J. suddenly spat vigorously at the splattered spittoon on the floor near his desk, missed, and came within an ace of hitting the gray cat with the three white paws and funny-looking eyes. Sweet William, the cat, let go a screech of rage at the indignity of having one of his white paws splattered with tobacco juice. Charging at the far wall, he turned and sat on his haunches with his tail curling around him, its tip still in warning movement as he glared venomously back at the person in the chair, who didn't even notice him.

J.J. sighed, wondering what Slocum was up to. He supposed he'd located Cullen about now, and was out at Millicent's. Millicent, of course, was four-square on the side of the maverickers against the big men, and he knew she was in trouble. Bigelow knew the likes of Tyrell; he knew the companies for which such men devoted their lives. The sons of bitches were late-comers, arrived on the gravy train when men like himself and old man Kincaid and such had fought the Injuns and tamed the land; and now they took over. Shit! He looked at Sweet William.

"Like you," he said aloud, his tone surly. "Take you in; and you take over! By God! Who the hell you think you are, getting all smart-assed when it ain't exactly to your likin'!"

Adjusting his hat, which never left his head, at least during waking hours, he tilted back in his chair, canted his head to the filthy window, and reckoned the hour of the day. Well, the best he could do would be to go through the motions. Damn! If he could've deputized Slocum he'd have gone at it straight. But alone . . . well, he'd have to see. Fact, though, he had been close to old Kincaid at one time. The old man had set up his brand about the time J.J. had left the country to work over around Laramie. That was before he'd become a marshal. But he'd always had a liking for Abel Kincaid, and what was extra, he'd favored that nice little wife of his too.

J.J.'s jaws began to work faster on his chew as he

thought of Lily Kincaid. Well, far as he knew, there'd been no hard feelings on the part of Abel. Abel, for the matter of that, had gotten the girl. There'd been nothing said, nothing lost. And he'd settled for Lucy. No regrets. Yet he paused now, leaning back in the round-backed chair, tilting on its rear legs as the long sunlight slanted in through the dim window, bright even so, playing on his gnarled hands and the side of his sixty-some-year-old face. That was this good while ago, and suddenly he sat up. And the past cut off from him like a roped calf who is busted pronto right on his ass.

J. J. Bigelow was all business as he stood up, opened the gun cabinet standing at the wall opposite the desk, and took out a scattergun and some shells. Then he took an extra box of ammo for his handgun, put it in his jacket pocket, and walked out of the office.

In the noonday sun, Sweet William sat licking his paw and now and again shaking his head fast as a fly buzzed him.

Suddenly, and totally unexpectedly, the snow started to fly. Being in the mountains, one had to expect it, but the days were well into spring and it was not welcome. It was especially not wanted because of that terrible winter. Yet shrewder observers knew it would not last.

The men in the Pullman car were not totally uncomfortable; though crowded, there was still room for a number of the party of twenty to stretch out. The majority, however, were addressing themselves to cards and idle conversation.

The Texans had been recruited down in Texas and had met Matt Kahane in Denver. The plan was simple. As

Sir Archibald had put it, the time had come for action. Under the leadership of Kahane, assisted by Red Weber, an expedition would invade the north country and simply serve warrants on the rustlers. Anyone resisting would be shot. The gunmen would be paid five dollars a day, with a fifty-dollar bounty on each dead rustler. Weber had bought horses in Colorado so as not to excite suspicion if anyone in Wyoming started working horses so early in the year. For, as Tyrell explained to the four members of what he had dubbed the "Special Committee for the Stockgrowers' Association," the plan had been in his mind for some time. Now it was time to put it into effect.

The expedition would be joined on the north fork of the Hanratty River by riders from the Box Circle who, along with Kahane, would guide them to the ground of operation.

In one of the cars toward the front of the train Matt Kahane sat smoking a cheroot. Immersed in clouds of smoke and his own thoughts, he didn't look up when the door opened and Red Weber walked in. The train was lurching along its uneven roadbed, and the red-headed man had trouble keeping his feet. But he made his way safely to a crate opposite Kahane and sat down.

"I've checked the horses."

"The question is, are we on schedule? They will be starting their gather any time now."

"We are on time. Engineer says we'll be at Clay Pass before midnight."

"Good enough." Kahane shifted in his chair. His feet had been bothering him and he'd removed his boots, and he realized now that his feet would swell and he was going to have trouble getting his boots back on. "We get there at midnight. Then we should make it up to the North Fork in another day."

"It is snowing," Red Weber said, and he grinned. "Course, it'll be just as bad going for them as for us."

"It is only a flurry," Kahane said.

Weber was about to argue the point, but with a second look at his companion's face he changed his mind.

"What's the plan?" he asked.

"We ride from Clay Pass up to the North Fork, above the Kincaid place."

"Near the Box Circle line camp?"

The big man's hard black hat nodded. He had not looked once at Weber, a fact of which the red-headed man was well aware.

"And then what?"

"We wait."

"Shit, Kahane, this bunch is right now getting feisty; they ain't going to like sitting around waiting up in those goddamn mountains in the snow."

"They are getting paid. They will wait," Kahane said, and his black eyes suddenly found the man seated on the crate. "We are following orders."

"Tyrell's orders. Huh!"

After a pause, and with his eyes in the distance, Kahane took a puff on his cigar, lowered it, and said, "For the moment. But just remember this, Weber. I am taking orders from Tyrell for the moment. But you—you are taking orders from me, and not just for the moment. Do you understand?"

Red Weber was no coward, but he didn't at all like what the other man was saying. Yet he nodded. There was something in those black eyes, and—yes, something in that empty black sleeve, and in the way he had more than once seen Kahane draw and shoot, scoring once right between a man's eyes, another time shooting off the lobe of each ear of a Mexican tied to a wagon wheel, the man all but dying of fright as he sagged into unconsciousness from the ordeal. Kahane was no man to go against unless you had that extra. Red Weber had been looking for that extra for a good while, but he had not yet found it.

He nodded, stood up, and walked out of the car.

9

In the big bedroom of the big house Sir Archibald, lying
in bed, stretched luxuriantly and then reaching over felt
the bare buttocks of the girl lying on her stomach at his
left. He smiled appreciatively as the owner of those fine
buttocks murmured with pleasure. He then reached out
with his other hand and caressed the fine silky hair between the legs of the girl on his right side. He smiled at
the high ceiling. Both had served him nobly during the
recent activities which, needless to say, were his favorite
form of indulgence.

"Natasha, darling, it must be getting on. And I'm
expecting company." The girl at his left raised up onto
her elbows, her long blonde hair cascading down as she
did so.

"Bunny, couldn't we have some more?"

The girl on his right stirred, lifting her knees. But just
as he turned toward her he heard something and, stopping
abruptly, rose—swiftly for such a portly man—and stood
totally naked beside the big bed. He listened again. It
couldn't be that late, but for some reason he was anxious.

This damn business with the maverickers was becoming a bother and he wanted only to get something settled with them. Perhaps it was word from Kahane's man at Jack Creek line camp, reporting on the group waiting there. Kahane himself had ridden in earlier in the day, filled with success and good news of the venture with the Texans, who were now at the Box Circle line camp, awaiting orders. Red Weber was in charge, and Sir Archibald expected things were going smoothly still. Why shouldn't they? And so maybe news had come. He hadn't seen Kahane all day, but supposed he would show up with a report that evening. After all, there wasn't much time till the small stockmen would start their roundup.

He turned now from the window and regarded the two women in the bed. It was still almost impossible for him to tell them apart. Only Roe, the nearest one to him now, who had been lying on his right side, had that little mark just alongside her delightful orifice. And Natasha had the mole under her left breast.

"Bunny, there's time, isn't there?" It was Roe who was pleading with him now.

Sir Archibald struggled with himself, and lost. "Let me think a moment," he said cagily, fishing for further overtures.

"What's there to think about?" Natasha laughed, bouncing up onto her knees and almost banging into her sister. "We are at your service, master!"

He loved it when they talked to him like that.

"Can we?" Roe smiled with the tip of her tongue showing between her wet lips. And she let her stark white body lengthen sinuously along the pink sheets. "Bunny, baby..."

Sir Archibald was a most willing loser when it came to willpower at times like this.

When the heavy knocking came, Sir Archibald was lying all alone in the wide bed. The girls had only just left. Had one of them forgotten something? But it was clearly a man's knock; hard, dominant. Who? Damn! He had given precise orders never to be disturbed in the bedroom except in the case of severe emergency. It had better be a severe emergency, he decided, as he felt the clang of alarm, irritation, and challenge in his body.

The knocking started again while he hesitated. Now he called out, "Who is that?"

"Kahane!"

The single word brought a flush of anger to Sir Archibald's jowls as he rose and pulled on his dressing gown, and stepped to the door.

Matt Kahane stood alone in the open doorway, his hard face even more white than usual beneath his hard black hat.

"It is Slocum."

"What do you mean, it's Slocum? You mean they have brought him? Why the devil are you banging on my bedroom door when I've issued strict orders—"

"He got away from them."

"He got away! Had him and he got away from them! What are you saying? Stop that damn cryptic frontier talk. Tell me what has happened in clear, simple, intelligent English!"

He stood there before the slab-like figure of Kahane, furious and impatient.

"I am telling you," Kahane said evenly. "Red Weber

and Wagner and Graves tried to bring him in like you ordered."

Sir Archibald's lips pursed as he released a soft, nearly inaudible whistle.

"And what happened? Damn it, man, tell me!"

"I don't know yet. I will by God find out."

"I want a full report on what happened!" Tyrell snapped. "God damn all of you bloody fools!"

During the conversation Kahane had followed the Englishman into his office.

Sir Archibald Tyrell stood now in heavy anger at the large window overlooking the meadow, and beyond it, the willow-lined creek.

"I want to know what happened with those bloody fools," Tyrell repeated.

"Your guess is as good as mine," the man beside him said. "But I'd guess they just fucked up." And Kahane's face twisted in a malicious grin as he felt the Englishman's discomfort.

A long silence fell. At length Tyrell turned from the window. His big face was composed now as he said, "He will be firmly with the Kincaids now. We must act quickly." He moved to the big desk and sat down.

Kahane moved closer and remained standing, his black eyes on the bridge of his employer's nose.

"How close to the Kincaid place do you think the Texans are?" Sir Archibald raised his head to look not at Matt Kahane, but at something in the middle distance, the plan that was forming his vision.

"I'd say pretty close. I'm aiming to get out there to meet up with them; give them their orders."

"Yes, you had better." Sir Archibald Tyrell's words

were vague; his real thoughts were on something else. Kahane sensed this, for he looked at him hard.

Sir Archibald leaned forward, his belly folding around the edge of the desk as he laced his thick fingers together and laid his eyes right onto the other man's cold face. "I don't want that fool Weber making any more mistakes. I don't want anyone making mistakes, Kahane!"

"There will be no mistakes."

"We have not a moment to lose now. I want this thing settled—and immediately. And I want Cullen—dead or alive."

"And Slocum?"

"Slocum, I am informed, is an old war companion of Cullen's. It's rumored Slocum was a guerrilla; and maybe Cullen was too. The importance there is that they very likely don't take prisoners. And so neither will you!" Sir Archibald unfolded his fingers and laid both of his thick palms on the top of his mahogany desk. "Now then. You have the Broken Hat Ranch; and at the same time..." He emphasized his words with a slap on the desk. "... At the same time you will also wipe out the cabin across the valley."

"Millicent's?"

"Where Cullen is, if he is alive. And if he isn't..." Tyrell looked down at the backs of his hands. "I want those papers, Kahane. I don't care what you do to get them!"

At the Broken Hat tempers were nubbed tight, for the business at hand was serious; nobody could indulge in anger now, or horseplay. The gather would begin in the morning and trouble could be expected. Indeed, trouble

could come at any moment now. Boone had warned it.
And Boone invariably was right. He was right about the
weather.

"It'll fair off shortly," he had said when Ives had
voiced doubts about the suitability of snow and slush for
running a gather.

"It-it's g-g-go-going t-t-t-to b-be r-rough," Denny
stammered into his tin mug of coffee in the early dawn
as he sat with his brothers in the log cabin.

Kelly sniffed, picking his teeth with his fingernail.
"Rough or not, it's the way to do 'er. Shit, we can't sit
here waiting for the Association to come pick us off."

"P-p-pick us off?" Denny's eyes were big and round
as he regarded his brother. "Y-y-you m-m-mean..."

But Kelly didn't wait for him to finish. "They'll by
God drygulch us, or run in a big lynching party and
stretch us."

"Uh-uh!" snapped Boone. "Correction! They will *try*
to backshoot us or lynch us. *Try!* God damn it, remember
that!"

Ives grinned. "Got to remember we are four against
the whole of the Association."

"Wh-what a-a-a-about the-the-the others?" Denny
asked desperately.

"The rest of 'em in the valley ain't worth much more'n
a bucket of cold piss," Boone snarled

"But we need 'em, Boone," Ives said. "Don't forget
what Paw said—to work with the others—otherwise the
big outfits'll split and divide us and pick us off single."

"I know that, you dumb shit!" Boone's scowl took
over his whole face. "I know that. We are working with
them. I just say what I said to you. Fact is, they got
some good men with them. But they are slow. They take

too much time with their goddamn thinking and like that. We got to act."

"But they're agreeing with us now, Boone," Kelly pointed out.

"Fin'ly, yeah!"

He stood up, tall under the overhead lamp, and, reaching up, turned down the wick so that the gray light of dawn could enter the room through the small windows.

"We'll check the stock, me and Kelly. Ives, you and Denny feed the hosses."

"I-I-I c-c-c-can d-d-d-do th-that." Denny stood up, his cheeks coloring.

"He can do it, Boone," Ives said. "Let him, and the three of us can check stock better."

Boone hesitated. He had seen the hurt in his young brother's face at being singled out for supervision, tying up a man.

He didn't say anything but simply turned on his heel and clomped out of the cabin, which meant he agreed. Boone never, never voiced agreement. On those rare times when he lined up with someone else's view it was done in silence; still his way.

The sun was up over the rimrocks when Ives and Denny followed their brothers to the barn. At one point Boone stopped and squinted across the valley toward Millicent's place, while his brothers followed suit.

"Wonder what happened to that feller," Kelly said.

"S-S-Slo-c-c-cum," Denny said. He stood beside his three brothers, his neck still sore, thinking of the man who had saved him from a lynching. "I-I-I h-h-ho-hope he-he c-c-comes b-b-ba-back."

"He likely won't," Boone said. "He was looking for Cullen. He'll be careful not to get caught up in that man's

151

business—whore stuff and the like."

"Cullen's a good man," Kelly said. "He done right by us when he was sheriff."

They had continued toward the barn, and Boone nodded. "That's sure. But he is trouble. That kind calls out trouble. I know the type. You'll see."

Denny watched his three brothers ride out, and he knew that Boone wasn't too set about it, but hadn't gone against Kelly and Ives. This time. He was glad. He knew Boone liked him. No doubt there. But he was too protecting, too careful with running the family now with Paw and Maw gone. For a moment the boy stood in the barn door remembering his parents.

He made a perfect target for the man with the Winchester.

Slocum heard the Winchester as he rode out of the big stand of spruce and pine just below the Broken Hat. It reverberated along the high rimrocks and down through the valley, carrying into the soughing silence it had broken. Now, only the wind.

It was easy enough to read. It wasn't an animal that had received that bullet. In the silence now, he knew that the war had started.

He didn't hesitate, but quickly booted the blue roan up the trail, and in not many minutes he was riding into the flat area by the spring box, with a full view of the horse corral, the sod roof of the log barn, and, beyond, the cabin. He drew rein, studying the ground ahead, listening. But there was nothing. There was no one. Whoever had fired that shot would be gone. Or waiting for another? Not likely. Not if, indeed, someone had been bushwhacked. The killer wouldn't wait around for seconds.

As he rode in now, he saw the small body lying just outside the barn door, and knew instantly who it was. Denny Kincaid looked almost tiny as he lay sprawled on the hard ground. As he squatted beside the still warm body, listening to the calling of a jay in a nearby tree, John Slocum felt the stinging in the backs of his eyes, and the anger filling him.

By the time Boone and his brothers rode in, he had already found the killer's tracks and was putting together what had happened.

"You know who it was?" Boone asked, forcing the words past tight eyes and lips.

"He was big, he wore trail boots, and he chewed tobacco. He came in from over there. Ground-hitched his horse, so he was well broke. Horse had a loose shoe on the front left, but he wasn't lame or anything. A big animal." He held up a tuft of hair. "Sorrel, still with some of his winter coat coming off. And I'd say the man was left-handed."

"How you know that?" Boone cut his eyes hard and fast to the side of Slocum's face, while Kelly and Ives held their eyes on their dead brother.

"He favored that side. See those prints, how he walked." Slocum spat thoughtfully, canting his head and squinting at the sun. "The son of a bitch . . ." He said it thoughtfully, the word carrying no anger. They were all of them far beyond the anger of a word.

"We will bury him by the spring," Boone said. "Denny used to sit by there sometimes."

"It's your action," Slocum said. "But I do believe I'd

put him in the icehouse for now."

"Why? Why you figure that?" Ives asked in hard surprise.

"It wasn't chance, this here. It was planned. It had to be. So they'll either be coming, or they'll be waiting for you to lose your heads and attack them."

"Bullshit!" said Kelly. "We'll plant Denny and then we'll settle with the bastards!"

Slocum looked at the three men, each in turn. "You'd better listen. Where are the rest of the cattlemen? Your bunch?"

"We're starting the gather this day," Boone said. "They'll be riding the range, picking up whatever they come across."

"And they'll be easy targets, just like this." He looked down at Denny.

Ives took off his jacket and laid it carefully over his brother's head.

"I'll kill every one of those sons of bitch bastards!" snarled Boone. "You say a sorrel horse, Slocum. You sure that red hair ain't from a red-bearded son of a bitch name of Weber?"

"It's horse hair. But those prints could be Weber's. But you want to be sure. Listen!"

He held up his hand as all of them heard some rocks falling in the timber above the ranch.

"Hear that? They're coming in over the rimrocks."

"There's no trail," Ives said.

"You've been over there, I'll bet or you wouldn't say there wasn't a trail," Slocum insisted. "That's how they're coming in."

And they listened again to the sound of small rocks rattling down from the timber line.

"We'll be ready, by God!" snapped Boone, and he turned back to his horse.

"Wait!" Slocum's single word had the strength to hold them where they were. "We have got to think clearly. You boys are all feisted up; now you wanted me to throw in with you. Denny was a friend of mine. I want you to listen." He eyed each one carefully. "We don't know but what they could have a helluva lot of guns. So we've got to move fast."

"He is right," Boone said. "Damn it. There's three of us only, least till the rest of the boys come."

"Four," Slocum said. "Don't you never listen, Boone?" It was an attempt at humor to lighten things, imitating Boone's famous impatience, but the Kincaids were too hard into their brother's murder. Yet Slocum saw that he had their attention now.

"Don't reckon any of you boys ever fought the Sioux or any other of the Indians," he said now. And, not waiting for an answer, he swept on. "We'll try an old Injun trick; we'll decoy them."

"What you mean?" Kelly asked.

"They're not after the cattle. They want to wipe you all out, and likely myself as well. Tyrell wants the valley, and he is planning on taking over Cole City to boot. He also wants Cullen, and I mean real bad."

"I thought it was Weber mostly."

"And Kahane."

"It is Tyrell," Slocum said, "and them too. The point is, they won't stop here. Maybe they even have enough guns to make a double attack, across the valley and here at the same time."

"So what you want us to do?" Boone said.

"One of you—Boone—get the message to the other

outfits who're in the gather. The rest of us will wait till they get closer, and we'll decoy them down into the valley and across to Millicent's, which is tougher to get into than here. I mean, they can't come in from above. We'll stay just out of range of their guns. We'll lead 'em back up to Millicent's. Meanwhile, Boone will have the boys waiting there in ambush, ready for them."

"By God, we'll do her!"

"Then haul ass; I mean right now! And get the boys over to Millicent's. Kelly, you ride down along the side of the east trail, and Ives down the west. I'll go down the middle."

"There's no trail there," Kelly said. "It's real steep; the way to hell."

"That's what I know. Now move yer asses. First get Denny into the icehouse and hid. Quick!"

They were just in time. They all heard the yelling as they were sighted, though fortunately Boone had gotten well away. Bullets began to thrash the air around them as they turned their horses and, splitting in the three directions, the way Slocum had indicated, raced down and away.

The regulators followed hard after them, also splitting their forces. Kahane could be heard yelling orders. Slocum too was again calling out to Ives and Kelly to keep just out of range of gunfire, but not to go too far. They had plenty of room for maneuvering, plus the advantage of knowing what they were doing. Besides, their horses were in better condition than those of the regulators, who had struggled over the rimrocks and then down the mountain.

Slocum was only concerned that Kelly or Ives might let their anger take over and charge into a closer fight, but he saw that his idea had caught on with them. They were taking to the tactic naturally. Gradually the three of them worked down to the river, firing back at their pursuers only when they were sure the shot would tell.

It was risky, but he had learned the tactic years ago from watching Fire Hawk and a tiny band tease a whole company of soldiers from Fort Winton, leading them right into an ambush from which not a single white escaped.

What was so vital now was Boone's getting the maverickers together and well placed at Millicent's for surprise crossfire. They were working closer to the river now, and there was the delicate question of picking the best place to cross, but the Kincaids knew the terrain well, and Kelly was shouting to him where he should maneuver.

The sun was halfway down the afternoon sky when Slocum and the two Kincaids forded the river. Finding cover quickly, they kept their rifles trained on the crossings. It was a good moment. It was a damn good moment, for the regulators were struggling to find their way across and had trouble with their horses, who were tired from their long ride. Slocum shot two out of their saddles, and Ives and Kelly settled three more. But there were still nearly twenty left, for, though they didn't know it, Kahane had added most of the Box Circle's gunmen to the Texans.

Yet there was something missing, Slocum sensed. It was always the way with professionals when the going got tough. You needed more than money to fight with all your guts. It was what made men like the Kincaids so tough—their spirit. Still, the numbers could break them.

By now the three of them had drawn further away from the river as the Texans and the Box Circle men struggled across on weary, frightened horses.

Gradually Slocum and the two Kincaids began to work their way up the long draw that led toward Millicent's, quartering their mounts back and forth, seeking cover whenever it was available, and firing at the oncoming regulators.

At one point as he was reloading, Slocum, looking over at Kelly, saw him get hit in the shoulder, and almost drop his gun. But Kelly Kincaid simply changed hands. He never cussed or said a word. It gave Slocum a good feeling, and he remembered the courage he had seen in Denny's face when he'd sat the dun horse waiting for his neck to snap.

They were almost at the level of Millicent's cabin now, and he looked up to see if there was any sign of activity. Seeing none, he shouted to Ives that he was heading up to check the situation. It was going to be a hell of a note if Boone hadn't gotten there yet with the rest of the maverickers.

Breaking away now, he urged the roan up the last stretch to the cabin. Finally reaching the protection of trees, he drew rein to let the animal catch his breath. Blue was sweating plenty, and so, Slocum realized, was his rider. But there was really no time for a rest, and he kicked the horse into a canter as they broke into the open ground around the log cabin. As he rode up, he felt his insides go heavy, seeing not a sign of Boone and the maverickers.

Riding to the back of the house, he dismounted and wrapped the roan's reins loosely around the hitching rail. The gunfire sounded louder and he could hear the shouts of men. He knew that in only moments the regulators would have the cabin surrounded.

Quickly he stepped to the back door, which was opened by someone inside who had evidently seen him riding up.

"Greetings," said J. J. Bigelow, chewing rapidly on his cud of tobacco. "You got here right handy like."

10

J. J. Bigelow had a sour grin on his face. "Might say I am glad to see you, Slocum. Or am I wrong there? Was it you led them gunfighters up to this place, by God!"

"Denny is dead. Murdered."

"Jesus..." The word broke from J.J. like a breath knocked out of him.

Slocum saw the pain come into Rhonda's eyes as her hand touched the edge of her lips. She tried to say something, but nothing came out.

"That is what has been happening," he said, and he accepted the glass of whiskey Millicent handed him. "The war is on. They're just about here."

"They are here," Cullen said, his voice throaty at one of the windows.

"What the hell you doing up?" Slocum demanded.

"Gimme a drink, Millicent." And then, to Slocum, "Looking for Kahane, my friend. Looking for Kahane; and Weber too if I get a chance for seconds. But Kahane first."

"He the one drygulched you?"

"Can't prove it. But I'll bet all I've got right now, and that is my life. That is all I've got."

"Where's your silver flask?" Slocum asked suddenly.

"How the hell do I know! I guess it got lost in all the action."

"Did you have it the day you were ambushed?"

Cullen was standing in the middle of the room, wearing only his long-handled underwear with the flap door at the back half-buttoned. He looked like a strange bird, with his iron-white hair tufted up on the top of his head, his bony face spiked with gray whiskers; but with his eyes as bright as fresh whiskey. "I do believe so, now you mention it." He nodded in agreement with himself. "I do believe it."

The gunfire was rapid now, and Slocum said, "I'm going back outside. I'll be more help there."

"I'll go with you," Cullen said.

"No! You old fart, you stay right where you are!" roared Millicent.

"You and Bigelow hold this place. We have got men coming—if they ever get here." Slocum spoke quickly at the door. His eyes turned on the girl. He thought she had become even more beautiful. "You all right?"

"Yes—yes, I'm all right." And he felt something warm going all the way through him as he stepped outside and, in one movement, unhitched his horse and mounted. Just as a wave of bullets hit the front of the house he saw Kelly and Ives Kincaid riding fast across the little open place and into the line of trees.

"Split up!" he shouted. "One on each side of the clearing. We'll crossfire the front of the cabin."

Ives let out a Texas yell as he reached the trees. It

was just at this point that a crash of new gunfire broke into the mountain air, and he heard Boone's voice roaring orders on the far side of the clearing. He was coming up almost directly behind the Texans and the Box Circle men, who were neatly trapped. For a moment Slocum couldn't believe it had happened.

Still, it wasn't over yet. The Texans, driven to the wall now, were earning their pay, and so were the Box Circle men. Slocum felt the tug of a bullet at his sleeve and realized he'd been nicked. He saw one of Boone's men drop from a horse, his hands clutching his face. Another was shot in the leg, and the bullet must have burned his horse, who began bucking and finally threw him. But the regulators were having a rough time. They were boxed in and in a few moments they began throwing down their guns. And it was over.

Boone was grinning a hard grin when he rode up to Slocum. There was blood on his shirt. He'd been creased along the shoulder, but he rode his horse firm as a rock.

Suddenly a shout went up, and someone at the edge of the group pointed down the long drop into the valley. "There goes Kahane!"

"And Weber!" another voice called out.

Boone had turned his horse, but Slocum grabbed the reins. "Get your arm fixed first," he said. "He'll be around. There are a whole lot more men at the Box Circle, you can bet. The war isn't over. It's just begun. We'll get them—Kahane and Weber—and then it'll be done."

"And Tyrell?" Ives Kincaid said. "What about Tyrell?"

"Him too."

J. J. Bigelow had stepped to the front of the tableau

now, his scattergun in full evidence. "I want all them guns collected." He nodded to two of Boone Kincaid's men. "You gather 'em; Henry there and Clive. Stash 'em by that wagon. And you Texas sons of bitches, you ride on back to Texas or you'll by God be taking up residence in Wyoming—permanent!"

He turned to Slocum. "You won't take the law in your hands, you and Boone. I will talk to Tyrell and them other two. You mind me now!"

Boone started to speak, but Slocum touched his arm. "Let it ride, Boone."

Boone saw the sense in that, for he said nothing. In a little while the Texans and the Box Circle men had departed, taking their casualties with them, and the Kincaids had ridden back to the Broken Hat.

The long evening light washed across the rimrocks now and down through the timber and into the quiet valley.

"It isn't over," Slocum said when he walked into the cabin and faced Millicent and Rhonda, and Nat Cullen.

Cullen was wheezing, unsteady on his feet.

"The excitement has got the old buzzard," Millicent said.

"The sons of bitches still don't have them papers," Cullen said, and he cackled.

"Sounds like a drunk crow," Millicent said. "What papers you talking about?"

"Never you mind. You mind your own business." He glared at her and Slocum suddenly felt uneasy. There was a wild look in his eyes as he stood there weaving a little, holding his fingers to his chest.

And then, before anyone could do anything, he had fallen to the floor. Slocum kneeled on one knee and lifted him and carried him into the bedroom. He was wheezing, but faintly.

"Looks to be about it," J.J. said.

They could see that Cullen was trying to say something. His lips were working, but no sound came out. Slocum bent close to him, trying to pick out a word or two, his ear right up to Cullen's mouth.

"What's he saying? You make it out?" J.J. asked when Slocum straightened up.

Slocum didn't answer. All of them watched now as Cullen suddenly stiffened all over his body, then lay still. No one said anything. Only a little sob broke from Millicent. No one had to say Nat Cullen was dead.

They left Millicent alone with him then, and went into the other room. J. J. Bigelow poured whiskey for all of them.

"He wouldn't go in the root cellar," Rhonda said to Slocum. "He insisted on being in on the fight."

"The root cellar?"

"That's where Millicent used to hide him when anyone came by who looked suspicious."

J. J. Bigelow approached with whiskey then, as Millicent came out of Cullen's room.

"He say anything you could hear?" she asked Slocum.

"Nothing I could make out," Slocum said; and he felt J.J.'s eyes on him.

He had again decided to bed down out by the timber line. It was a cool night, the sky thick with brilliant stars and stardust. He lay on his bedroll going over what had happened, planning ahead to the morning when they would dig a grave for Cullen. He had realized when the fighting had ended that Kahane had used only a few of the Box

Circle gunmen, that the bulk of the force had been the Texans. Clearly, the fight was by no means over; there would still be a strong Box Circle force to go against the roundup. Not to mention scores to be settled with Kahane and Weber and, yes, maybe even Tyrell.

He had told Boone and his brothers to get going on the gather with their fellow stockgrowers, that he would see him after some business he had to attend to on Cullen's behalf. The boys had ridden off, swearing vengeance on whoever had murdered Denny.

"We could track him, Slocum. I mean, you know his prints; you had a good idea on the son of a bitch," Boone said.

"I could. And I will. But first get your beeves together. Otherwise, Denny will have been wasted; you'll give up your roundup and branding, and that's what Tyrell wants."

They saw the sense in that, though reluctantly, for they were eager to wreak vengeance.

"I'll dig him out," Slocum promised. "And I'll turn him over to you."

"You will?" Kelly said.

"I said so."

He had watched them ride off, realizing that the Kincaids and their friends had about as much chance against the Chelting Land and Cattle Company as a man pissing into a hurricane. There was only one way to go now. Right to the core. Right to Tyrell. Right to Kahane and Weber.

He had slept, for he knew the moment of coming fully awake when he heard her step, then saw her as she approached in the clear night.

"I hope I am not disturbing you, Slocum." He was aware of the catch in her breath as she spoke.

"You are disturbing me," he said. "It's the kind of disturbance I favor."

She sat down on the edge of his bedroll and he remained on his back, looking up into her face. She was wearing the same perfume she had in the stagecoach, and as she inclined her head toward him now a brown lock of hair fell down over her forehead. Slocum felt his erection spring up as he reached up and slipped his arm around her.

Her whole body melted against him as his lips found hers, softly, gently, searchingly. Her breath came quickly now as he drew her all the way down beside him.

"Slocum . . ."

"What?"

"Can we go slowly?"

"I wouldn't think of any way except the way we both want it," he said.

"Thank you," she whispered.

He was helping her with her clothes now, then opening his bed so that she could slip in beside him, taking his erection between her thighs. His hands fondled her high, firm breasts. They were young, eager, springy with youth and desire, with large nipples that right now were as hard as his penis.

"Oh, Slocum, I want you so much! So much!"

"You've got me," he said. "I can't hold you off any longer."

"Please don't joke."

"I wasn't, really. I want you too."

She pressed her lips to his, her mouth opening and her tongue meeting his tongue in delicious assault as her legs parted and she drew them up. Reaching down, she guided him into her, raising her hips to aid his entry. She was soaking wet, and he felt her on his thighs and belly, her wetness exciting him even more.

Now they began to move slowly, their bodies sealed together, but in no way hard or rigid, soft, and not hurried though eager. He thrust deep and she spread her legs even wider, now wriggling as the end of his great shaft touched bottom and she cried out in ecstasy.

He stroked her slowly, increasing just a little as she gasped and clung to him; but, to his great joy, entirely mobile.

He had no desire to change position, nor had she. It was perfect, and in this way they stroked to an exquisite climax.

"God," she murmured. "Oh God, it's so good. You've absolutely filled me!"

"It isn't over," he whispered, as he started moving his hips again while his organ grew once more to its full length.

"I can't believe it!" She almost cried out aloud as the joy seized her and now they were both pumping rapidly, their buttocks bucking in a faster and faster rhythm; at one point he was almost losing her, but recovering in the last inch to drive down and in and up high once again to her scream of delight as they came together, and kept coming, and coming...

They lay side by side, their hands entwined, silent, resting. Until again—and their timing was perfectly together—their passion rose and possessed them totally, maniacally now as they bucked and rode to the total emptiness that came with their united climax, as her legs tightened around him and he drove his ever-bigger member right up into the middle of her; and, pumping and gasping in their beautiful rhythm, they exploded.

His awakening was as silent as the coming dawn; he felt
as sweet as the land around him. The roan was cropping
the short buffalo grass nearby, and Slocum lay still for
several moments listening to the breaking day. Presently
he rose, rolled his bedding, and walked to the cabin for
breakfast.

Rhonda cooked—hotcakes and coffee. J. J. Bigelow
had stayed the night, but he was as silent as Millicent.
When breakfast was finished they went outside and, on
a little knoll overlooking the valley, Slocum dug the
grave, declining J.J.'s offer to help.

When it was all done, when Cullen was in his grave
and the words had been said by Millicent and the earth
shovelled back in and rocks placed so that it wouldn't
be dug up by animals, they all had a drink.

It was still early in the forenoon when Bigelow took
his leave, and a short while after Slocum saddled the
blue roan.

"Wanted to have a look at that root cellar," he said
casually to Millicent.

"It's yonder. Got that willow in front of it so it can't
be spotted unless you know it's there."

It was only a few yards from the back of the house
in the side of a low cutbank. There was a coal-oil lamp
hanging from a beam and Slocum lighted it. A small
room; he had to stoop. There was bedding for Cullen
when they hid him there against suspicious travelers who
might be interested in his whereabouts.

Quickly he searched the bedding, felt around the dirt
walls and on the dirt floor for any places that would
indicate a hiding place for papers or other valuables. But
there was nothing. He stood hunched in the low-ceilinged

room, puzzled. He was absolutely certain that when he had bent over Cullen as he lay dying he'd heard him say the words "root cellar."

He heard the step in the doorway. "Thought it might be in here," said the familiar voice.

"I have been expecting you, J.J. Why, I left the door open."

J.J. stepped farther into the little room, also having to bend because of his height. "Not a helluva lot of room in here."

"Enough for Cullen to hide out."

"And to hide whatever it was Kahane and Tyrell was after." The marshal spat suddenly on the dirt floor. "Figured they were just a little bit too strong in trying to find Cullen. I mean, I could understand Weber wanting to lay him by the heels on account of his woman. But them other two—shit, it had to be something extra. Something important."

Slocum turned to face the lawman now. "What do you figure it was?"

J.J. spat again on the dirt floor, canted his head, and pushed back the brim of his Stetson hat with his big forefinger. "Something he told you when you bent over him."

Slocum grinned at that. "He said 'root cellar;' at least, that is what I heard. And I reckon you heard it too."

J.J. nodded. "Sounded something like that, now you mention it." He spat again directly on top of his previous glob of spittle. "Nothing, huh?"

When they were outside Bigelow said, "You will be riding to town, I reckon."

"I reckon."

"I am here to keep the peace. I don't want you or any

of the Box Circle bunch shooting up the place."

"I wouldn't think of it, Marshal Bigelow."

J. J. Bigelow looked directly at him now, his eyes thin, his lips tight, as though he was dealing with something real sour.

"You look like you got a lemon up your ass, J.J.," Slocum said genially. "Take it slow. I won't bring any trouble to town."

"Mebbe. But whatever it is Tyrell wanted from Cullen, he will figure you got it now. And I might be startin' to figger that myself. So you watch it." He walked briskly to his horse and stepped into the saddle. Looking down, he said, "And I will be watching you."

"And them?"

"And them."

"Just remember what they did to Denny Kincaid."

"You want to take on as deputy, Slocum?"

Slocum had to smile at that. "Tell you what, J.J., I will turn it over. I will study it and let you know."

"I do appreciate that," the marshal said, his words pulled all the way out of him like a cork from a bottle of vinegar.

Slocum watched him ride off then. He waited, smoking a quirly, while he thought over what had just happened, wondering what Cullen had meant by his words, for he had put him on a wrong track. Or maybe it had only been the incoherent babbling of a man about to die.

He waited for J.J. to get well ahead on the trail, and then he started in to Cole City himself. He had ridden well into the middle of the forenoon when he realized somebody had cut his trail. Seeing a cutbank up ahead and near it a big clump of bullberry bushes, he kicked the roan into a gallop. When he had reached the bushes and the cutbank he drew rein, dismounted, and pulled the Winchester out of its scabbard. He had a clear view of the trail and he was nicely protected.

He wasn't too surprised when he saw Boone Kincaid and Ives and Kelly cantering toward him.

"So to hell with the gather?" he said, stepping out into the trail.

Drawing rein, Boone looked down, grinning wickedly. "No, it's going to be to hell with Tyrell and Kahane and that red-headed son of a bitch whose name I don't want to say since it makes me puke!"

"What about the gather, you dumb shits?"

"The boys are doing fine," Kelly said. "We have come to see this one through. Don't want you getting snotty and taking Kahane and those bastards for yourself. We want our justice, Slocum, by God!"

Boone said, "Bigelow came by to keep his eye on the gather. He has got that scattergun to handle anybody with a notion to argue." And then he added, "We planted Denny."

Slocum looked at the sun, reading the time of day. "Then we don't want to waste time setting here and picking our noses," he said. He slid the Winchester back into its scabbard and mounted the roan.

In the hot sun the four of them rode quickly toward Cole City.

Colonel Quimby Hounds sat in the Can't Lose Saloon perusing the latest edition of the Cole City *Finger–Gazette*. He was actually engaged in more than mere perusal; he was avidly reading a story which he had written himself and chuckling with appreciation at its humor, its wit, its choice of vocabulary, and its clear, ringing thought.

Quimby Hounds appreciated those fine qualities he attributed to himself. At the same time, he realized he had his weaknesses. One of these was Millicent, the lady whose favors he had purchased more than a few times. And so he was both surprised—in fact, astonished—and wholly delighted when the lady walked into the Can't Lose and, seeing him, came over to his table.

"Millicent!" The colonel bounded to his feet, almost tripping against the chair leg, but recovering to take her hand in both of his. "To what do we owe this surprising visit?"

"Get me a drink, for Christ's sake," Millicent snorted as she sat down in the chair Hounds offered.

"It'll be whiskey, will it?"

"The good stuff, not that trail shit they pass off!"

"But of course!" The colonel flew to the bar and in a moment was back with a fresh bottle and two glasses. "I shall join you. This brand being . . . uh . . . more suitable, as I am sure you will agree." He removed the bottle he had been drinking from, placing it on another table as though it was at least slightly poisoned—which it might have been.

"What are you doing in town?"

"I came in with Rhonda. She's over at the San Francisco House. I have business."

"Business?" The colonel's cheeks and jowls, his forehead, indeed his entire body fell into silent gravity as he said, "Ah—I heard. I heard the terrible news."

Millicent was silent. She reached into a large pocket in her jacket and took out a cigar.

Swift as a gunhawk, the colonel offered a light, the flame lighting up her determined though stained cheeks. "We are preparing an obituary for the *Finger–Gazette*,"

he said gravely, his gray tone of voice in complement to
the funereal heaviness of his slender body. At that moment he looked close to being a corpse himself.

"Where is Slocum?" Millicent said, opening up a little
under the release offered by the booze and the cigar.

"Slocum? I haven't seen him. Didn't know he was in
town."

"He was riding in." Suddenly she looked directly at
Quimby Hounds. "There's gonna be big trouble. I felt it
the minute we came in. Tyrell and Kahane have got this
town pinned. I saw some men on the rooftops and some
others in the alleys."

"That is what I know," Hounds said, lowering his
voice to a rasping whisper which carried for several feet.
"A person would do well to stay home on a day like
this."

"That's what I see," Millicent said. "The street is
about deserted. I'm glad I got Rhonda in the hotel."

"You should be there too."

"And yourself?"

"An old codger like me—it doesn't matter. When it's
your time, it's your time. Of course," and he cocked his
head engagingly to one side as his blue eyes twinkled
across her face and then her bosom, "I would indeed
miss you, my dear."

"Bullshit!" Millicent said, and closed her eyes in vast
appreciation of her cigar.

Neither she nor her companion had given more than
a cursory glance at the man slumped in a chair against
the far wall of the saloon. In the extremely dim light,
with his Stetson hat low on his forehead, he appeared to
be asleep. Neither of them had spotted John Slocum.

• • •

He had left the Kincaids at the creek below Cole City, and had then ridden into town with hardly a disturbance of the atmosphere, the horse's hooves barely stirring the dry street to dust. The street was pretty much empty: a team and wagon outside the general store, a packhorse at the smith's, and outside the Pick-Em-Up four saddle horses. He recognized Matt Kahane's big buckskin stud.

He had his plan, and it did not include the Pick-Em-Up. He rode on down to the San Francisco House and took a room. It was mid-afternoon when he walked down to the Can't Lose Saloon and Gaming Hall.

Now he was well situated in semi-darkness with the wall behind him and an expanse on either side so that he could maneuver. What he couldn't see directly he could catch in the big mirror behind the bar. He had been watching Hounds and Millicent for some time, wondering what the girl was doing there, though suspecting it was because of Cullen. The colonel, of course, was a regular patron.

He could feel the tightness of the town; he'd seen the men on the roofs when he'd ridden in, and others in the alleys. Well, he had his plan. And, hell, it *was* the Can't Lose Saloon, wasn't it?

Looking over at the squeak of the swinging doors, he saw the two men enter. Each wore a tied-down sixgun. They stood just inside the doorway looking around the room, their hard eyes stopping on Slocum.

When they reached his table Slocum was leaning close to it with his empty hands out of sight. "I have got a goosegun pointed right at your four balls, and I got a twitch in my finger. What do you want?"

Their color had changed all the way up to their hat-brims and he saw the tightening in their bodies.

"Kahane wants to talk to you, Slocum."

"Tell Kahane it is just as far from me to him as it is from him to me." He kept his eyes right on them, but they didn't hold the moment. They turned and left the room.

"Good Lord!" exclaimed Quimby Hounds from the other side of the room. "It is Slocum!"

"They coming back here for some gunplay?" Millicent called out, getting to her feet.

"Where is your sister, Millicent?" Slocum said.

"I hope she's still at the San Francisco House."

"You better get back there and stay with her."

"You are alone?" the bartender asked Slocum guardedly, as he came back into the room. He was a thin man with a totally bald head.

"You are here," Slocum said mildly, and the man paled. He went quickly out of the room again, wiping his hands on his apron.

"You better beat it, Colonel."

"I . . . uh . . . perhaps you are right, Slocum. News is news, to be sure, and I do need eyewitness reports, but from the living. I don't know how to communicate with the dead." Rising swiftly, he started out of the saloon.

"Git along, Millicent! This ain't your fight."

"I'll be at the hotel with Rhonda."

Slocum watched them leave. Then he got up and changed his position to the opposite side of the room. Now there was only himself. In the dusty silence he listened to the ticking of the big clock hanging on the wall across from him.

After several moments he heard a movement on the other side of the door through which the bartender had left, and Boone Kincaid walked in.

"Where are Kelly and Ives?" Slocum asked.

"Covering the back door in the alley. They got horses."

"Good enough."

"I'm still going to whip the shit out of you, Slocum."

"No, you're not," Slocum said as the batwing doors swung open and the two Box Circle gunmen who had delivered the message walked in, followed by Red Weber and Kahane.

For a split second their attention went to the side of the room where he had been sitting before, when they'd delivered their message from Kahane. It was enough to give Slocum and Boone the edge. As the gunmen swept to the edges of the room Slocum fired, drilling the left one in his leg, while Boone dropped Red Weber with a slug right between his eyes. The second gunman was firing and Kahane had leapt to the far side of the room, throwing lead, which nicked Slocum's thigh. Boone meanwhile took a bullet in the fleshy part of his left arm where he'd been wounded out at Millicent's, yet he gunned down the second Box Circle man. From the floor the Box Circle man shot the gun out of Boone's hand before falling dead on his face.

Suddenly Kahane holstered his gun and raised his one arm. "My gun's empty, Slocum. You wouldn't shoot an unarmed man, would you?"

"Oh yes I would. If you move an inch you are dead, Kahane!"

"I hear you. You have won, Slocum, for the present." The hatred and fury in Kahane's face was engraved in each line. Slocum hadn't seen a man like that in a long time.

"I haven't won for the present, Kahane. As far as you're concerned I've won forever. You had better know that!"

But there was something wrong. He could feel it. He looked over at Boone, who was pulling himself into a chair.

"It was Weber drygulched Denny, wasn't it, Kahane?" Slocum moved his Colt in emphasis of his question.

"That is correct. Not acting on my orders, the dumb bastard!"

"Boone, you got the son of a bitch right between the eyes."

"Isn't that enough, Slocum?" Kahane's voice had a hollow ring in it.

Slocum still had that strange feeling in his guts. He would have bet his life that the gambler's gun wasn't empty. And indeed, he realized in the next moment that he was about to do just that.

Suddenly a crisp British voice broke into the devastating scene.

"Don't move! I'm afraid you haven't won a thing, Slocum." Sir Archibald Tyrell appeared from behind two more Box Circle men who had entered the room; he was covering Slocum with a Smith & Wesson. Slocum could see the Englishman clearly in the big mirror behind the bar. Tyrell's gun was pointed right at his back.

"Drop your gun, Slocum. I have you dead to rights. And, as Mr. Kahane here will tell you—if you ask—I can shoot the arsehole out of a running pack rat. With either hand. Easily!" He cleared his throat. "Drop your revolver!"

"I have Kahane covered."

"Tyrell!" Kahane's face was ashen.

"Slocum, drop your gun!"

"I will holster it," Slocum said, and the words fell like dealt aces as he slipped the Colt into his holster. "If you shoot me now it will be cold murder, Tyrell, and you'll never get your hands on those land grants."

Quimby Hounds, who had crept back to the swinging doors to get an eyewitness account of the fight, felt a shiver go all through him as he saw Tyrell's face go almost blue-white, like a fish's belly. But, for some unbelievable reason, Sir Archibald Tyrell took it. Already writing the story in his mind, the colonel put it to Slocum's outrageous audacity. The room itself seemed to Hounds to have a special sting in it now. *By God,* he was thinking; and for a moment he felt that it was Slocum who had Tyrell under his gun, and not vice versa.

It was when he saw Kahane shift his stance, with his eyes going behind him, that Slocum realized the big man was looking at Tyrell. He could see in the mirror that he was in direct line between the two men, and in a flash he realized what each was up to; that he was only one of Kahane's targets, and also only one of Tyrell's. In the mirror he watched Tyrell's eyes shift to Kahane as the gambler's hand swept to his holstered sixgun.

In that instant of a single breath Slocum dropped to the floor, drawing the Colt and shooting Kahane in the lungs. Then he was rolling and twisting, firing at Tyrell. In that same moment another shot rang out and the Englishman clutched at his head as he fell to the floor. Looking up, Slocum saw Millicent with the Colt in her hand, her wild eyes on the dead Tyrell.

"That was for Nat, you son of a bitch," she said. And then she added, her voice almost a sob, "I dunno if it was me hit you or Slocum. But it's done. I'm only sorry

I couldn't get Kahane too, on account of it was him pulled the trigger." She stood now over the dead Kahane. "You son of a bitch, shooting a man when he's buttoning his pants!" And she shot the corpse right between the eyes.

11

The sunlight was throwing the shadows of the trees on
the bank of lush grass and on the water of the little creek;
like feathers, Slocum thought as he stepped down from
the spotted pony. He had taken Blue back to the livery
and picked up his own horse. He was glad to have the
spotted pony back, though the roan had served him well.
Now, after scouting the country a moment, he lay down
on his stomach and drank from the creek. Lying on the
rocky creekbed, he was aware of Cullen's flask pressing
against his chest. He had taken it from Kahane's pocket
after the shooting. The horse had taken a few steps into
the water and now drank, while the creek burbled against
his legs.

When Slocum had his fill he stood up and, taking out
a quirly, lighted it. It was then he saw the horseman
coming along his back trail.

He waited, standing swing-hipped in the hot forenoon,
a smile ready behind his impassive face. And when he
felt the friendly nature of J. J. Bigelow's greeting, he let
the smile out.

"Heading out to Millicent's, are you?" the marshal asked.

"Might."

"Wondered if you might of had second thoughts on whatever it was Tyrell and Kahane was after."

"Not that I could put a word to."

"It'll be all busted now, whatever it is," Bigelow said. "So it don't matter all that much."

"It'll be a rough time for a while, letting things settle."

"That is what I know." The marshal was chewing slowly, deep in thought. "Figured you was heading this way when I seen you taking off."

"How is Boone?"

"He'll be just fine. Says he owes you one."

"One what?"

"I reckon that is between you and him. You want to take on as deputy, Slocum? I sure need a good man to heal the wounds right now. I'm riding over now to watch those fellers branding. I am of course meaning the Kincaids and them."

"You got a good man, J.J. His name is Bigelow." With a nod, Slocum swung up onto the spotted pony. "So long."

He took his time. He was pretty sure Bigelow wouldn't follow him, though he knew the lawman was still suspicious that he knew something about why Tyrell was so anxious to get Cullen. But there was no sign of the marshal on his back trail.

Still, there was something in his mind that he couldn't fit together. Cullen had told him about the papers. And he was sure he'd been trying to tell him where they were hidden when he'd said the words "root cellar" just before he died. But he had searched the place, and so had Bigelow, and there was nothing.

It was mid-afternoon by the time he rode up to Millicent's place and saw the horses. He had allowed plenty of time for the two women to get there ahead of him. If asked, he'd have been at a loss to say why, but he somehow wanted it that way. He wanted to see the girl, for one thing.

When he swung down from the spotted pony, they both came out of the cabin to greet him.

"Come in, have some coffee," Millicent said.

"That's a good offer, lady." And he met the warm silence of Rhonda's soft brown eyes with his whole body opening.

"Christ," said Millicent when they were seated, "it looks like the gather is going to come off. The boys will get their brands registered, and there'll be peace in this country for a goddamn change!"

"Stop grumbling," Slocum said. "Why don't you and Rhonda take a trip someplace? Go to Kansas City, San Francisco. See the world."

"Might." Millicent's dour expression vanished. Her eyes lighted up. "By God, that could be!" She grinned at him as he reached into his pocket and took out Nat Cullen's flask.

"Thought you might like to have this," he said. "Kahane had it."

"Kahane! Then it really proves he drygulched Nat."

"Not that you didn't know it."

"Course I knew it. The son of a bitch was bragging it all over town. I've got ears." She picked it up, looking at it casually. "He used to keep this out in the root cellar, I remember, case he got stuck out there when he was hiding and hadn't got anything to drink. Course, every so often he'd go out there and have a nip too when I cut him off here. For his health, I mean."

"In the root cellar!"

"What's the matter?" Millicent stared hard at him. "Something the matter?"

Slocum was studying the bottom of the flask. "See this? See these numbers?"

"I ain't blind. I see them."

"Well, they're faint. They're just lightly scratched."

"What do you think they mean? Just numbers." She passed the flask to her sister.

"It isn't a date, I don't think," Rhonda said. "Just numbers."

"Think maybe it's a box in the bank? I recollect Cullen mentioning a feller named Tolson, from the bank."

"He is dead," Millicent said.

"Cullen thought he might have been killed. But he knew about the land grants, the papers that Tyrell was after. That's meaning that's where the flask was, or he thought it was, because I'd asked him about his flask. I'd seen Kahane drinking out of it."

Millicent sat back in her chair, slapping her hand on the bare table top so hard the coffee cups jumped. "Well, I'll be whang-danged!"

She was staring at him in amazement, with her mouth hanging open.

"I take it these papers, whatever they are, are valuable," Rhonda said, touching the flask with her finger.

"You bet."

"What'cha going to do now, Slocum?" Millicent asked.

Instead of answering her question he said, "Those papers show the best property to get hold of before the railroad spur comes to Cole City."

"Didn't ever hear of a spur," Millicent said.

"Those papers are worth a lot of money to the party who knows how to use them."

"Like Tyrell and the Chelting Company."

"Or anybody else."

"So what are you going to do?" Millicent asked again.

He looked at her. "You'll be moving out of here, won't you?"

"I dunno. Might." She turned to her sister. "Rhonda's been after me. But I don't know. You said take a trip."

"You could begin with that."

He felt Rhonda's eyes on him, feeling over his face. And at last he turned to her. Her eyes seemed even larger than they usually were.

"What will you do, Slocum? What . . . ?" She dropped her eyes to the silver flask lying in front of them.

"Those numbers have already caused a helluva lot of trouble," he said and he stood up, picking up the flask. "It's Cullen's, isn't it." He shook it. "Almost empty. Millicent, fill 'er up with your best merchandise and we'll just slip this in there with him right now."

"In the grave, by jingo," said Millicent, almost jumping to her feet.

"Hell," Slocum said. "A man never knows. He could have a need for it."

He had waited for her, out by the timberline, and then had fallen asleep under the clear, starry sky. It must have been late when he heard her leaving the house. In only a minute or two she had slipped down beside him.

"Slocum, I want you more than I've ever wanted anything."

"That's the best way to have it," he said.

185

"It might have to last forever."
"Each time it's forever."
"Let's make it last forever now."
"It's the only way," he said.

JAKE LOGAN

THE VOW

The Story of
One Man's Determination
to Obey God

Hal Donaldson
and Kenneth M. Dobson

Foreword by G. Raymond Carlson

The Vow
Hal Donaldson and Kenneth M. Dobson

Printed in the United States of America
ISBN: 1-880689-00-6
Copyright 1991, Onward Books, Inc.

Cover design by Matt Key

All Scripture quotations are taken from the *King James Version* of the Bible.
